I0645616

The Last Ferry Left at Five
by Günter Wendt
Translated by Rachel Reynolds and Stephanie Jaeger

Originally published in 2017 under the title
"Die letzte Fähre ging um fünf"
by Ahead and Amazing Verlag, Ostenfeld, Germany.

Published in the U.S. in 2023 by Auguste Crime,
an imprint of Clevo Books.

Clevo Books
530 Euclid Avenue
Suite 45a
Cleveland, Ohio 44115
www.clevobooks.com

Library of Congress Control Number: 2022947377
Paperback ISBN: 978-0-9973052-8-9
eBook ISBN: 978-1-68577-001-3

Printed in the USA
Cover and interior design by Ron Kretsch

First American Edition

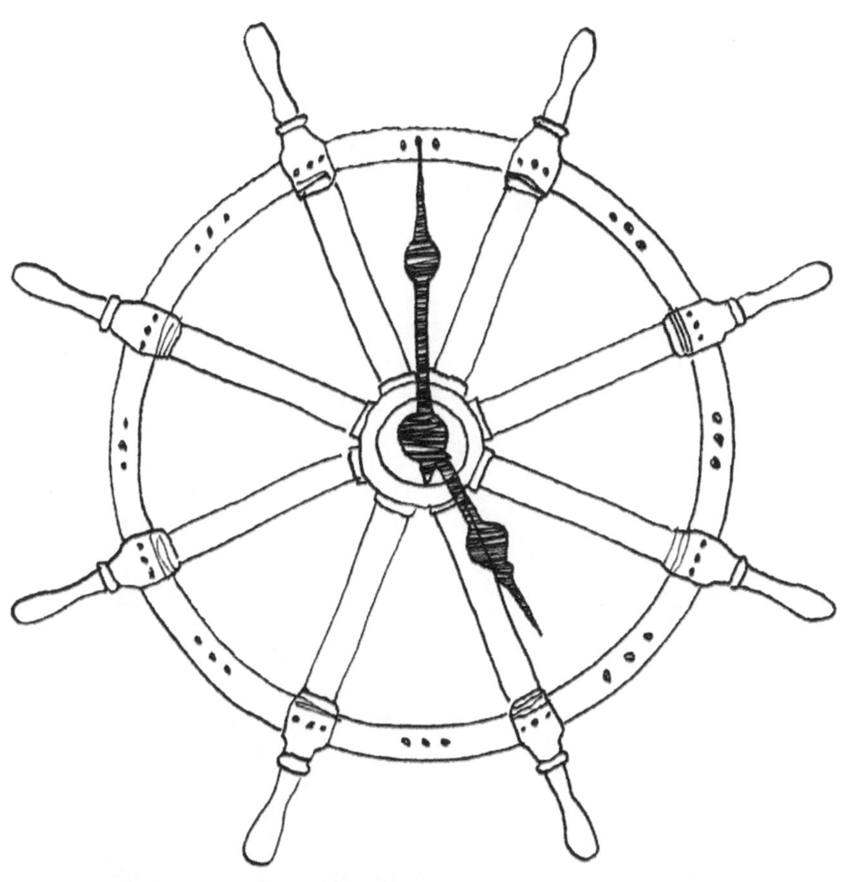

the last ferry left at five

günter wendt

translated by rachel reynolds
and stephanie jaeger

Dedicated to the inhabitants of the halligs.

ON THE FERRY
One day before the storm
5:00 p.m.

THE SMALL FERRY SANDCRAB PLOWED THROUGH the waves of the Wadden Sea, heading for Grienoog. Captain Hauke Ehlers, who was also head of the Carstens Shipping Company, was in good spirits. As he joked with one of the other officers, he increased the speed so that the sea water sprayed high across the bow.

Glorious weather! Sunny, seventy-five degrees, and wind speed between 4 and 5 knots from directly ahead.

Concerned, the other officer directed his gaze through the windshield toward the bow area, where vacationers were shouting and dashing for cover from the spray. Neither the wind, nor the waves were the problem. He was always more worried about the passengers sitting inside, the ones unsure whether they would die or just barf up their guts.

"Captain—shouldn't we slow down just a little...?"

"Hogwash, my girl can take it!" Ehlers cut him off. At almost eighty, he never missed his daily opportunity to steer the Sandcrab from Husum to Amrum. This was his world; he knew his way around it. At sea, all you had to do was keep an eye on the equipment—that was it. And accelerate, of course. Full speed ahead! In the past, he'd had only a compass, a radar and a map, with which to do drive the boat. The autopilot did most of the work these days, leaving only the casting off and docking to be handled manually.

Sometimes Ehlers wondered if the ship could reach its destination all on its own, remotely controlled by satellite or software. That was forbidden by the powers that be, however. At some point in the distant future that might change. For the time being, though, he was quite all right with the fact that ships still needed people to operate them. He shook his head inwardly. If things did get to that point, sea voyages would no longer be fun; they would be as dull as dirt. Once he was no longer able to plow his boat through the Wadden Sea at breakneck speed, the fun would be over. The Coast Guard had his number on this count, and he had already been fined several times. His fellow crewmates always looked a little piqued whenever they heard that "the old man" was back on the bridge. The end result tended to be broken dishes, vomiting guests, and a bruise or two on those passengers who had drunk one too many beers since boarding time.

The ship skipped across the waves, thundering through the water, dipping deep, and continuing on its raucous wave ride. Ehlers knew exactly what he could ask of his "crab." He could feel it in his gut. Experience had taught him that.

"Grienoog," he announced laconically, before the others had even caught sight of the hallig through their binoculars. By now, his crew were used to this. In the 1970s, when Ehlers had first started running his ferries, people had always frantically pressed their binoculars to their eyes. No, he couldn't be right. But he was! By this point, they had grown accustomed to the fact that ten minutes before arrival, their boss would declare that this or that hallig or island was up ahead. This time was no different.

Life came crackling through the loudspeakers. An employee of the shipping company alerted the passengers that they would reach their destination shortly, and ended the announcement with the obligatory instructions for the upcoming docking maneuvers.

A tired man in a black leather jacket sat on the upper deck. No longer quite so young, but not too shabby either. Graying at the temples, he had a three-day beard across his cheeks, and a braid dangled from the nape of his neck. His legs were clad in faded jeans, his feet in blue sneakers. Next to him sat a large leather suitcase that had seen better days, in addition to two yellow shoulder bags made of tarp material on which the logo of some shipping company could be seen.

The ferry was still performing its final maneuvers when the gangway crashed down on the wooden planks of the jetty. With a groan, the man rose to his feet, straightened his jacket, grabbed his suitcase and shouldered his bags, then squinted into the sun.

He pulled out a damaged cigarette and stuck it in his mouth.

"Herr Kollerup!" the on-board speakers croaked indignantly with a pinch of reproach, "We're here."

The man directed his gaze to the ship's bridge and waved to the impatient officer, before leaving the ferry as the last passenger on board. Behind him, the gangway was cranked up with a loud rattle, and the Sandcrab shot on toward Amrum.

Chief Inspector Kollerup, head of the Husum homicide department, dropped his suitcase and lit his cigarette. He stood in the wind with his arms outstretched and his eyes half-closed, his braid fluttering slightly. This was like a hallig out of some movie: lush green grass speckled with sea lavender.

A bright white haubarg stretched into the sky on a nearby mound. Several structures with thatched roofs stood scattered across other mounds, and there were no trees except those right around the hotel. Low shrubs and bushes, bent by the steady wind, dominated the barren landscape. Above everything stretched a deep blue, cloudless sky across which swallows flitted back and forth. Shit! He thought. It's awesome here! He sat down on a bench at the jetty and smoked his cigarette. All this peace and quiet!

Only then did he realize how much he'd needed this vacation. At the moment, there wasn't much of anything going on at home in the Husum homicide department. His colleague Larsson could manage the little bit of work they had right now. Besides, this vacation was free for him. All-inclusive. He had won first prize in a competition held by the Husumer Tageblatt newspaper. He could have brought a guest with him, but since he hadn't had a steady partner for years and hadn't wanted to take anyone else with him, he had leaped at the chance when he was informed that he could stay for three weeks if he came by himself. What he saw here exceeded all expectations. He had thought he would find himself in a small, musty-smelling boarding house when he had read that the first prize was a stay at the Hotel Deichvogt located on the Grienoog Hallig.

He smashed out his cigarette and shuffled toward the hotel. With each step, his fatigue started to fade.

By the time he reached the main dwelling mound—it was farther from the jetty than it had seemed—he was all sweaty. And it was higher than he'd thought it was. A flight of stairs led to the entrance, reminding him of the song "Stairway to Heaven." Thank goodness he'd been met by an employee. The young man greeted him with the words, "Moin. Already here? You should've buzzed me from the dock, then I could've picked you up with the Smart car."

"Buzzed?" asked Kollerup.

"Yes, with your phone. You could've used the app you got when you booked..." The young man trailed off when the detective showed him his ancient flip phone. "Oh... I didn't know there were any of those still around." Incredulous astonishment.

"I left my work phone at home." Kollerup shrugged. The porter then grabbed his suitcase and sprinted up the steps. Minutes later, the panting police officer found himself in the foyer as well. A pretty young woman greeted him with a smile.

"Moin, Mr. Kollerup! I'm Nele. Welcome to the Deichvogt!"

"Moin." Well, things ARE off to a good start, Kollerup rejoiced inwardly as he filled out the check-in forms.

HOTEL
The day of the storm
10:00 a.m.

THE FIRST MORNING AT THE DEICHVOGT HOTEL greeted Kollerup with a sunny day that promised warmth. His room faced west, and he was glad he hadn't taken the room across the hall. The sun's probably beating down on that room, he thought, wishing the guest in there all the best. The rooms to the south were bound to be worse off, but thanks to air conditioning, it might still be bearable in them. With a sigh, he stood up and almost cracked his head against one of the roof beams: a rustic room. Modern and airy, but still rustic. He opened the dormer window and inhaled the fresh North Sea air. He bent his knees to get the night's kinks out and put the first cigarette of the day between his lips, but hesitated before lighting it. Who knows what they've installed up here? There might be hidden sprinkler systems with built-in cameras, and the manager himself would probably smash in the door with an axe to save the supposed fire victim. He leaned way out the window and took several hasty puffs on his cigarette.

It seemed to be a beautiful summer day. The steel blue sky and glassy water stretched out forever in front of him. A light, lazy breeze, barely noticeable, wafted up to him the scent of salt, summer flowers and grass. Kollerup was almost ashamed to desecrate this air with tobacco smoke. It was so quiet that he could feel the hum of a coaster vessel's engine as it headed for some destination along the North Sea coast.

With his cigarette butt in hand, he hoped the hotel's thatched roof was flame-retardant. He tamped out the embers in the gutter underneath his window and flicked the rest away. He couldn't see where it landed because the trajectory ended below the edge of the roof, probably in one of the flowerbeds that had been planted around the hotel. It didn't matter.

He stood for a long time in his high-end, fancy shower, trying to figure out how to get the water to turn on. Aha, push here, pull there and then... no. So pull there and turn here... a blast of ice-cold water made him gasp, though it didn't come from above, but from the wall itself! Hey, the shower's broken! He hit a red button, and his legs were suddenly being massaged by a high-powered jet of hot water.

Completely tired out and with soap suds still in his hair, he emerged finally, having managed to clean himself at least halfway decently after struggling with the unruly shower. While the exhaust fan sucked out the steam with a weak and steady inhale, he fumbled in the mist for his towel, snagging first a washcloth, then a hand towel. The bathroom mirror was very large but fogged up so badly that he couldn't see anything in it. He tried to rub it dry enough so that he could see sufficiently to finish getting ready, but it was in vain.

Exactly ninety minutes later, a fresh Kollerup was standing in front of the breakfast buffet.

Only a few guests were milling about in the restaurant area, which was open to the outdoors. Tables were set out on the terrace, where several guests were already seated. Kollerup loathed the "Weathered Look" that was spreading like a virus through many hotels along the North Sea. Pale gray and white furniture, sanded down several times and half-heartedly painted several more times. The end result were pieces that looked like they had seen decades of use. Or was it called "Country House Style"? Either way, it looks shabby, he decided. Like those ripped jeans you could buy for a ton of money. He examined what the dish in front of him had to offer. Everything your body didn't need, even down to those awful little sausages and, of course, bacon! Who could eat burnt meat in the morning? He shuddered inwardly as he watched a fellow guest scoop a mountain of scrambled eggs onto his plate. The world might end tomorrow—or worse—so I'm going to make the most of today!

Eventually Kollerup sat down at a table with four respectable rolls and some jam. Precisely measured butter, enough for eight halves, and a mug of coffee were strategically spread out in front of him as well. In honor of this fine morning, he had also indulged in two slices of cheese. With jam, it was pure poetry! He sipped his coffee with relish.

Crap! Someone should have prepared him for this cup of "sock-to-the-kisser good-morning coffee." It tasted like it had been roasted with a welding torch. He raised a hand and ordered a cup of "decent drip coffee and not this sludge."

After breakfast, he strolled through the hotel, past the bar, which was aptly named the Harbor Bar, and the fitness room, which he ignored. The next stop was a tiny souvenir shop, which was more like a cabinet packed with keepsakes from the North Sea. A pile of "North Sea stones" lay there, remarkably similar to ones he had once seen advertised in Switzerland as "authentic mountain stream rocks." Picture postcards and other junk that the well-heeled guests could take home rounded out the display. A bicycle rental desk sat next to the souvenir stand. Kollerup found this a little extreme. Bikes on a hallig! But there were always suckers out there willing to pay ten euros for ten minutes of cycling. That was it for the first floor, except for the kitchen and the hotel service areas. Taking the hallway that connects the small foyer with the back of the hotel, Kollerup strolled out through the southern exit, beyond which stretched an elaborately replenished beach and the Wadden Sea.

Ten beach chairs were scattered across the sand, looking rather forlorn. It was only shortly before noon, but the air was already quite hot. The yet-unfurled sun umbrellas, stylized palm trees with plastic leaves, hung limply on their posts.

Kollerup had seen similar things on postcards. The scenery was interchangeable, whether you were on Mallorca, or by the Aegean, the Mediterranean, or the Pacific. The entrance to the beach sported a sign written in spidery script. Chill Zone, it said, funnily enough. A bar, which also appeared to have been lifted from some South Pacific decor line, stood deserted, without a bartender. Elevator music, or lounge music as it was called these days, trickled out of hidden speakers. "Stairway to Heaven"... some awful kitschy version with a piano. Not my world, Kollerup decided.

He decided to take a walk around the hallig, and this took him about an hour: past the pier, desolate now at low tide, along a sheep pasture. He should have brought some water with him, he groaned inwardly. He couldn't stand this heat! In the newspapers in the hotel lobby, the weather report had predicted a mild breeze for today with a high of ninety. Too hot for this area! Out in the channel, among the other halligs and islands, he could see white dots floating out in the heat like a mirage: the ferries to the mainland and the islands. It felt like he was standing on some forgotten Pacific island, unnoticed and undiscovered by the rest of the world. With his leather jacket over his arm, he crested a small hill and looked around.

The hotel, the employees' residence, and a small structure, also situated on a low mound, that he thought was probably a sheepfold. Off to the side stood an old church whose tower had apparently been demolished, and next to it a miniature golf course with little cottages. This was the small, green hallig world.

The name fits, he thought. Grienoog: green eyes.

In front of the cottage stood an easel with a half-finished painting on it: an industrial landscape. He glanced around. Who would look at this island and see a devastated landscape blighted by belching smokestacks? He leaned over and studied a detail: a dead sheep with a vulture hovering over it. Or a crow. That was probably up to the viewer's interpretation. Kollerup decided it was a swallow, giving in to yearning to find at least a hint of the beautiful world before him.

"Onne!"

Kollerup wheeled around. "Huh?"

A bearded, rather squat man stood in the doorway of the cabin, grinning ear to ear. Shorts, short legs, and a grubby undershirt, a bottle of beer clutched in one hand.

"Onne, that's my name. And what's yours?" The bearded munchkin held out a paint-smeared hand to him.

"Uh, Kolle." Kollerup shook the paw offered to him. "Kollerup, actually, but my friends call me Kolle."

"Moin, Kolle. I'm Onne." Onne pointed the bottle toward the hotel. "A guest?"

"Yeah."

"Money?"

"Nope. Prize."

"Sweepstakes?"

"Yep."

"Beer?"

"Cold?"

"Yep."

"Sure."

"Give me a sec."

The man rattled and clattered around the cabin before returning with an ice-cold bottle.

"Cheers!"

"Cheers!"

The silence that followed was broken only by gurgling gulps and a bleating sheep.

"Kalle's stressed again." Kolle looked up questioningly, and Onne pointed his bottle at a sheep. "That fat one." An obviously overweight sheep with dark brown, almost black fur was standing in front of a fellow sheep and snorting belligerently. Then he took off and crashed his skull into his opponent's. The ensuing crack sounded like two coconut halves slamming hollowly into each other.

"Kalle!" yelled Onne.

The ram in question glanced their way and shook his head as if to say, "That guy was just asking for it!"

"Get outta here, or I'll turn you into mutton shanks!"

"Meeehee!" bleated Kalle, before trotting indignantly to the water trough, where he proceeded to chew his cud and drown his sorrows.

"Your sheep?" asked Kolle.

"Nope. I just make sure they don't bash each other's heads in. In exchange, I get to live here."

"What do you do?"

"I'm a painter."

"That one?"

"Yes and others. Want to see some?"

"Uh..."

"Wait."

He emerged staggering out of his hut with several pictures, each as tall as he was, and tossed them onto the grass. Kolle was startled; brown and black dominated everything, speckled with bits of green and orange. Gloomy pictures, all of which utilized this hallig as a motif, though the theme seemed to be "destruction by industry": black wind turbines dripping blood; dead sheep; crows, vultures or swallows tearing at the carcasses. One painting had a drill rig as its central subject, from which brown sludge shot up into the sky and straight into the face of a pale white sun.

"Nice," Kolle said tersely.

"Nice, really?" Onne gazed morosely at his artwork. "We'll be facing shit like this all too soon. Want another beer?"

"No thanks. It's too early."

"Come on inside," Onne urged him.

The cabin was quite spacious and disorganized, though the furnishings were modern and remarkably dust-free. Despite the fact that the once-red exterior paint was peeling and the asphalt shingles were already mossy, the interior was clean and freshly painted. The laminate on the floor looked brand new, and the space was divided up by a kitchenette, a bed, a table on which lay cutlery and hotel dishes, and next to it a chair. On one wall hung a flat screen television, and an air conditioner roared in a corner, working against the rising heat. "Can't stand the nights otherwise," Onne admitted with a grin when he saw Kollerup's astonished look.

The walls were covered with the pictures Onne had presumably painted in recent weeks. However, these differed from the ones Kolle had seen outside: sunsets in a North Frisian landscape, wispy clouds floating weightlessly over salt marshes where beach lilacs bloomed, nice houses on the edge of sandy cliffs with cheerful people playing ball on the lower beach. The thirty-square-meter interior instantly grew a little brighter, and you could literally smell the sea mingled with the scent of the salt marsh in summertime.

Onne was able to move around upright inside the cottage because of his short stature, but Kolle had to stoop some. After busying himself in the refrigerator and availing himself of his second beer of the day, Onne belched self-consciously and apologized for the mess. "My maid hasn't been in yet," he said laconically and seemingly in all sincerity. Unprompted, he explained that he was allowed to stay here for free because he looked after the sheep, which belonged to the hotel. "That's what people want." He spat out the word people with marked disdain. "Sheep, wind and sea." At that, he squinted at Kollerup.

"Meh, I can do without that."

"Where are you from?"

"Husum."

"I see. I'm from Schobüll."

"That counts as Husum too."

"Schobüll is still Schobüll." Onne was alluding to the incorporation of the village of Schobüll into the town of Husum a few years previously; it hadn't been a very popular move with some of the Schobüll natives. After rummaging around in a cupboard, he showed Kollerup a photo: a large house and nice garden and a flat expanse of land. Schobüll at the water's edge, no dike.

"That used to be mine."

"Not anymore?"

"They seized it."

"Why?"

"For an above-ground power line from Nordstrand and Pellworm. They have to get the power to the mainland somehow."

"But you were paid for it."

"Only a fraction of what it was worth, but I don't want to complain. There's still some left over."

"Wife and kids?"

"Yes, they live in Hamburg now."

"Divorced?"

"As fast as you can fart," Onne confirmed. "As soon as the money was in the account, they were gone."

"Where do you live in the off-season?"

"Are you a cop? Why are you asking so many questions?"

"Yes, I am, but that's irrelevant." Kollerup pointed to the pictures on the walls and said, "Nice pictures."

"A cop. So..."

"Uh, yeah. Listen, I need to get going." Kolle was embarrassed that he'd fallen into his old pattern. He was on vacation, for crying out loud.

"What exactly do you do on the police force?"

"Homicide detective, but now I really have to go." He was about to turn toward the door.

"Wait a minute!" Onne's friendliness evaporated as his features hardened.

"Yes?" Kolle looked at him, though he already knew what was coming. Uncertain, Onne glanced at the door and peeked through the windows for a moment. "You have to help me." That was as far as he got.

A voice called out his name. "Onne? Are you there?" It was apparently the maid. He rolled his eyes and shouted a response at her before turning back to Kolle.

"We'll talk about it tomorrow," he whispered. "It's urgent!"

"Ah, Svenja! Moin!" he greeted the young woman cheerfully. In walked a petite, red-haired young woman who also had to hunch her shoulders slightly upon entering the cabin.

Dressed neatly in white slacks and a hotel shirt, she smiled broadly and called out a loud "Moin, you two!"

While she cleared away the dirty dishes and loaded them into her electric cart, Kollerup lit a cigarette in the shade behind the cabin and listened to Onne joking with Svenja through an open window, as she changed the bed sheets and cleaned the small bathroom. When she was done, she whirred away in her electric vehicle.

"Hey, Onne!" called Kollerup. Armed with brushes and palette, the artist rounded the corner. "Gotta paint now," he announced curtly. Kolle joined him at the easel: another brownish black doomsday picture. This time a dead man lay stretched out in front of a building, which bore an unmistakable resemblance to the island hotel.

"What exactly did you want to tell me?"

"It's not that important."

"That's not what it sounded like."

"Tomorrow."

"All right, that's up to you. I'm going over there to check out the church."

"There's not much to see there; it's a sheep stall now."

"Oh yeah? Well then..."

"There's not much to do here."

"Have you ever exhibited your paintings anywhere?"

"Yes."

"Where?"

"Oh, New York and stuff."

"Really?" Kolle had a hard time believing that paintings like this could sell like hot cakes. But art is art, he thought.

"Yes, but not these."

"Which ones?"

"Some older ones."

"What did you paint before?"

"Abstract pictures, feelings as shapes and colors."

"I see."

Feeling like he had overstayed his welcome, Kolle said goodbye to Onne, who was now standing in front of his canvas with a furrowed brow, completely absorbed and twirling his brush like crazy.

Since it was already past noon—Kolle hadn't noticed how quickly the time had flown by—he returned to the hotel. Time to see if there's anything edible besides mussels and fish, he mused. On the asphalt path, a bike practically hit him.

"Hey! Watch it!" he shouted after it, but the cyclist had already sped around the corner of the hotel. Unbelievable! But then again, why was he getting all bent out of shape? He was supposed to be on vacation.

There were only three guests in the restaurant, but Kolle ignored them and sat down at a table near the door out to the terrace. Nope. Better outside. He got up and took a seat underneath an umbrella, just as a gentle breeze stirred and intensified the feeling of being targeted by a giant blow dryer. It was cooler inside because the air conditioner was on full blast, but since he was a smoker, he had to face the heat in the shade. As he sat there, he let his thoughts run wild; that Onne was a strange one. While Kolle mused about the bizarre meeting with the painter-cum-recreational shepherd, the radio droned in the background. "The oldest and rarest-played songs of the 70s," the announcer purred, before "Dancing Queen" by Abba started playing. Rare? Kolle shook his head; unfortunately, this was only the single version. He glanced around. Someone had forgotten a tablet on his table, although strangely enough, each of the other tables also had tablets sitting on them. He picked up the flat, chalkboard-evocative artifact of modern society, and as soon as he had it in front of him, the display came to life.

"HELLO!" the text bellowed at him, then below that, a prompt: "If you would like to place an order, press ORDER now." He pressed ORDER. Immediately, a new text appeared: "Would you like food or a beverage? Or food AND a beverage? May we recommend tonight's menu to you? Please press the appropriate button." Several options were provided below this line, and he pressed EAT AND DRINK, at which a short list of lunch dishes appeared. The English word LUNCH headed what looked like a list of appetizers. Lunch? He sighed. Oh for the good old days when real meals had been part of the noon repast! But he didn't want to cause a scene; after all, he was on vacation! All inclusive. He opted for what they called a "tuna sand-witch" and a "chilled sheep with greens" salad, in addition to an apple juice spritzer. The cold beer from Onne was sitting heavily in his stomach. Once he made his selections, he had to enter his room number and the ten-digit code on his electronic room card. As a final reward, his device announced that his order was being processed. Kolle played around with the tablet some more and examined the evening's menu. Mainly fish: redfish and cod in ten different variations. The only non-seafood meat on the menu was beef, supposedly "salt marsh beef" in eight variations. Excellent! The evening was saved, he realized joyfully. For dessert, there was fruity ice cream or panna cotta, also offered in various iterations. And as typical in every hotel, a vast array of drinks were available. He didn't recognize most of the beers, but oh well, he wouldn't die of thirst. By the time he was done with poking around on the tablet, his food and drink had arrived. Apparently the hotel manager had hired all the beauty queens along the west coast of Schleswig-Holstein; his order was served by a real Nordic beauty: a blonde pageboy cut, freckles, and a figure somewhere between not too voluptuous and not too skinny. With brown eyes to boot. Unfortunately, she was gone too quickly. Time will tell, Kolle thought with a grin before concentrating on his lunch. In his day, people would have called what was sitting in front of him a snack. But what was "his day"? More like the 70s, when life had been more exciting. Well, it was still exciting these days too, but it lacked that trembling, inner turmoil. Kolle munched on his sandwich as "Sweet Home Alabama" trickled out of the hidden speakers, but then the music was interrupted by an announcement:

"We interrupt our program for an updated severe weather warning. Tonight the West Coast will experience heavy rain, severe thunderstorms with gale-force winds, and the possibility of tornadoes. The storm surge is expected to hit around 8 p.m. Please keep in mind this storm has already caused major damage in the British Isles. An unexpected tornado on the UK's East Coast has knocked out several power plants. At least ten towns have been without power for the past few hours. We will report back when more news is available about the expected severe weather."

Kolle gazed out at the North Sea. He thought about the fact that people tended to overreact when a storm was in the offing. He could see several day trippers heading off the beach, apparently intent on making their way back to the mainland. Whining children with exasperated mothers.

"No! You heard what the man on the radio said. And I want to be home by the time it starts!"

"But, Mom...!"

Kolle rolled his eyes. Had he actually been like that once? But, Mom! A useless protest at best. The waitress returned and cleared his table, then she taped a sign up on the porch door. "The terrace will be closed tonight. Thank you for your understanding." Kolle didn't care; he looked at his watch. It was siesta time. As he passed the bar, he caught sight of the TV: disastrous news from the UK. It all seemed rather blown out of proportion to him—agitated reporters were standing in front of the smoking remains of a substation. They were reporting on what had happened using trite, pathos-laden phrases about the damage and the potential number of injuries. The presenter asked the correspondent on site whether there were any fatalities, and you could tell from the studio broadcaster's face that he wasn't at all happy when the question was answered with a shrug. Apparently only locations along the East Coast had been affected. Since the local substation received some of its power from the offshore wind turbines and transported it inland, the power supply was going to be cut off for three hours. The turbines in the North Sea had been taken off the grid to prevent the possibility of increasing potential damage through overvoltage. The coverage then switched gears to the flooded areas of the marshes, which in this area faced the open North Sea without dike protection. Kollerup shuddered slightly at the thought of living so vulnerably, without a dike. Well, the people in the Husum district of Schobüll knew what that felt like, but for whatever reason, he felt completely defenseless without a dike.

Still in his clothes, Kollerup stretched out on his freshly-made bed. Despite the now scorching sun, it was pleasantly cool in his room. Was the haubarg storm-proof? Yes, it had to be, he reassured himself. After all, it had stood for several centuries without suffering any damage. The mound, with its height of almost ten meters, was also above any water level the highest storm tides could reach. As he imagined the haubarg floating off into the distance while the world sank into the depths, he slowly drifted off to sleep.

Someone was pounding on his door. What the hell was that about! It was the hotel manager, whose cream-colored clothes looked as if he had just walked off the golf course.

"Moin. Just wanted to make sure that everything is to your satisfaction."

"Yes, it is."

"Satisfied with the room?"

"Yes, I am."

"I also wanted to ask you if you would like to have dinner at the restaurant tonight."

"Yeah, like... yeah sure."

"Well, it's just that some guests have canceled their rooms, so I wanted to see if the chef needed to prepare for any special orders."

"Yeah, uh... special orders?"

"You know, when there are only five or six guests, the menu will have a smaller number of items, as opposed to when we have a full house."

"Oh, you mean because of the severe weather warning? Good grief! I'm from Husum, and a breeze like this doesn't bother me. So you can rest assured that I'm staying. And as for the food, I'm perfectly satisfied with roasted potatoes and some kind of meat."

The man seemed visibly relieved. He excused himself and was already knocking on the door of another room.

Cancellations, interesting. Kolle stood at the window and realized that it was already late afternoon, after four. He helped himself from the minibar, since it was close enough to five o'clock. I wonder what Onne and his sheep will do in this weather. That's right: the old church. Kolle set his empty bottle on the minibar, pulled on his sneakers, and went downstairs.

There was confusion at the reception desk because several guests wanted to check out, while others were desperate to know what the weather would be like tomorrow and whether the hallig was storm surge-proof. The young woman behind the counter had everything under control, assuring the guests that there was no way the storm would cause a storm surge on the hallig. Things would be worse on the coast itself, where the water could back up. The wind direction also made it very unlikely that landfall would occur here. Some waves would certainly reach the salt marshes, but everything would really just be completely normal and harmless. Besides, it would be low tide at the time the storm was predicted to hit.

Behind the desk was a door to an office, which was now open, and through it Kolle could see a middle-aged woman talking excitedly on the phone. He could make out some of what she was saying because she was talking so loudly. The subject of the conversation seemed to pertain to a mudflat hike that was supposed to take place the next day. The woman tried several times to calm down the person on the other end of the line. "Yes, well, I can't help it if some guests are leaving! I can't help the weather!"

Kolle left the madhouse and was amazed at how hot it was outside. There was no sign of the impending storm; the sky was a brilliant blue. After lighting a cigarette, he shuffled over to the circular path that skirted the perimeter of the hallig. Because of the outgoing tide, which in his opinion was particularly pronounced today, the mudflats smelled strongly of silt and salt in the brooding sun. To his left, he saw sheep grazing in the distance, with the old church behind them. A small dot was scurrying around and seemed to be trying to herd the sheep onto the church mound; that couldn't be an easy feat. He had to grin as he watched Onne among his sheep.

At the jetty, the Sandcrab was just mooring. A group of tourists was standing on the pier, anxiously waiting to catch the last ferry of the day to the mainland. The scene looked like an escape attempt from some impending catastrophe, in Kolle's opinion. Animals have a sixth sense when it comes to approaching storms, he mused. Perhaps some people retain this instinct to flee, while others don't. Just at that moment, a flock of seagulls passed by, hightailing it toward the mainland.

No sooner had the ferry left, at 5 p.m. sharp, than a small boat with an outboard motor came chugging up. A man disembarked, rather unusually dressed in corduroy trousers and a quilted vest; odd considering the weather, Kolle thought. The man carefully moored his nutshell of a boat, then noticed Kollerup up on the hotel mound. For a second, the man just stood there staring, so Kolle waved at him just for fun. No reaction whatsoever. The man picked up his backpack and walked over to the hotel. Kollerup assumed that this was probably the mudflat guide, who was coming to air his grievances in person. This definitely wasn't his problem, so he turned toward the beach.

A few guests were still lolling around on the loungers, sipping colorful drinks while reggae music softly burbled in the background. He recognized the song as "Whole Lotta Love" by Led Zeppelin. Not as reggae! He sat down at the imitation South Seas bar and snapped at the waiter.

"Tell me... who actually picks the music?"

"What do you mean?" the barkeeper grinned.

"That sappy drivel playing over the speakers is what I mean."

"Oh, you mean the lounge music!"

"Yes, exactly. That sludge some people call music."

"It's from some guy on the internet."

"What do you mean the internet?"

"It's coming from the internet."

"The music?"

"Yeah, it's internet radio."

The internet! Didn't anyone have their own CDs anymore? Kolle refused to even let himself think about LPs. Or what about an MP3 player at least? Kolle envisioned the music industry swirling down the drain. In an act of defiance, he ordered a drink called a "Swimming Pool." He had planned to ask the bartender for his personal drink recommendations, but if the music came from the internet and was selected by some faceless person, he didn't even want to think about what kind of drinks the internet would recommend for this weather.

He took a long sip of his cocktail, which was actually a

mixed drink, and then engaged the man behind the bar in a conversation about swimming pools and the colors of the bikinis women wore when swimming in said pools. And then they got onto the topic of climate change and hot summers. The guy behind the counter, whose name was Maik, was of the opinion that the change would prove to be good for tourism. Kolle disagreed, since global climate change didn't necessarily mean that it would suddenly become permanently warmer here. He referred to the warning that a storm was supposed to hit the West Coast tonight.

"Come on, severe weather?! What they call severe weather can't compare to a force 12 fall storm. And even those," the bartender pointed to the haubarg, "don't bother this old lady. Good, old-fashioned workmanship, absolutely storm- and storm surge-proof. However," he glanced up at the hotel, "we'll probably have to re-fill the beach after the storm."

Kolle suspected that this would be the lesser of the two problems. He thought about the sheep and Onne, and asked Maik about them.

"Oh, he'll join us tonight if it gets too bad." He waved off the concern. "Otherwise his hut is safe and sound, and high enough to handle a summer flood. He'll be just as safe as the sheep in the old church."

Suddenly there were loud voices behind him; someone was complaining about something or other, and then he heard, "I don't give a damn what happens! I won't let you shut me out like this! You will answer for that!"

Then a woman's voice: "What do you think I can do about a storm!"

"Oh, I'm not talking about the weather! It's the fact that you gave Frerk Carstens my tour! Mine!" The man's voice screeched. "There will be repercussions! Mark my words."

Repercussions? Maik rolled his eyes and whispered confidentially over the bar, "That's Kai, the mudflat guide. He's mad because the boss booked a tour with another guide, but that's fallen through now too."

Kolle glanced at his watch. Six o'clock. Wow, how time flies! He gave Maik his room number and went upstairs to take a shower.

Not too bad for the first day of his vacation, he thought. He had met someone interesting, but otherwise he had spent his day doing nothing even remotely related to murder or manslaughter. Sometimes he thought that humanity had lost its collective mind. The cases he had to deal with often made him doubt humanity's sanity, not because some were easier to solve, for there were hard nuts to crack as well, but because the motives never seemed to change even the slightest: revenge, greed, jealousy, envy, and so on.

He climbed cautiously into the shower, and very gently pulled the levers and turned just the handles that controlled the water from above. Someday there'll be voice-controlled showers, like in the science fiction movies, he thought. "Water from above, 74 degrees!" he called out as a test. He almost fell through the glass shower door when a female voice replied, "Now, if you'll just kindly say please, the water will start."

"Who's that?!"

"I'm your automatic shower setting—Betty."

"Please, I'd like hot water from above."

"Gladly. How many degrees?"

"74."

"The magic word?"

"Please?"

"In a complete sentence."

"Please, I'd like to have hot water at 74 degrees from above."

"At what pressure?"

"What are my options?"

"Hard, medium and gentle."

"Gentle?"

"Yes, for wimps and lightweights."

"Medium." He immediately realized his mistake and added a please.

"My pleasure. When you're done, press the stop button to

end the shower. I wish you a pleasant shower."

"Thank you."

"You're welcome."

After his shower, exuding the overpowering scent of the hotel's own hygiene products, he marveled at the black wall that was creeping in from the west, swallowing the sun. It abruptly grew significantly darker. He loved storms; those are the times when you realize you're alive, he would say whenever someone complained about bad weather. He could sit at a window for hours, and if possible, he enjoyed spending time outside in the tingling atmosphere that existed as a storm approached. The air always felt as if it were electrically charged, and the front-edge cloud formations with their yellow-black wisps were like the opener to some bombastic concert. "Thunderstruck" by ACDC was the song that came to his mind on these occasions. The same thing was happening now, as the wall pushed its way up into the sky. And it was oppressively humid as well. Kolle closed the window regretfully and went downstairs to the restaurant.

Nele, the pretty young woman he had seen at the front desk, led him to his table. The room was lit with candles, and soft music tinkled from hidden speakers. He seemed to be the first guest there. As he placed his order, in person and eye-to-eye with a human server, the tables filled with diners, although he didn't pay much attention to who was sitting where. Through the terrace door, they could admire the natural spectacle starting its second act. He seemed to be the only one enjoying it. Everyone else seemed to be shaking their heads, fretting about the danger and the possibility of fatal consequences. Kolle snorted contemptuously. Cowards!

His first course—iceberg lettuce with fennel—began to the accompaniment of lightning. The second course was applauded by pelting hail against the terrace doors. He agreed that the applause was justified. Even he, as an amateur chef, couldn't have done better. The first bite of steak was commented on by a roll of thunder that lasted until Kollerup swallowed his mouthful. His beer arrived, and his first sip was followed by a squall in its wake, which knocked over the outside bar. Ha! Splendid! Kollerup enjoyed the show. While the staff calmly strode among the agitated patrons to take orders or distribute menus, the weather got down to business. As the sun set over the North Sea, which the lightning occasionally flashed into his view, heavy rain showers could be seen drifting away. He glanced at his watch. Dammit! He had to get out of the habit of always checking his watch. Vacation, Kolle! It was now 9 p.m. Time apparently operated under its own laws here on the hallig. He burped as cautiously as he could, and then the light and the music went out. Kolle thought this was a bit of an overreaction to such a small burp.

A lady somewhere in the room squeaked, as a glass shattered sharply on the floor.

"Stay calm, ladies and gentlemen! The generators will start up any moment now!" a man's voice called out from somewhere in the darkness, and even as he spoke, the dining area grew brighter. Another flash twitched outside the windows, and a pale male figure appeared, pressed against the terrace door, where his bloody hands left thick red streaks on the glass as he slowly slid to the ground. The room then went black for a second time before another flash of lightning briefly illuminated the figure lying on the terrace. Kolle's intuition told him that this person was dead. A double thunder clap that made the glasses on the tables clink brought the scene to an end.

HOTEL
The day of the storm
9:00 p.m.

IF THINGS HAD BEEN A CHAOTIC MESS BEFORE, THE situation now grew dangerous. Tables were overturned, panic-stricken people shouted in confusion, children screamed, and glasses clattered and crashed. Kolle did what was always best in such cases: he remained seated.

Someone bumped into him, and he had to hold on to his table. He then pulled out his cell phone, flipped it open, and held it up high. It provided enough light for him to safely climb onto a table. Once upon it, he put two fingers in his mouth and whistled so loudly that the folks on Föhr hallig were bound to have heard it. In a split second, the room was as quiet as a mouse. "Everyone stay where they are! This is the police! Can the manager of this hotel hear me?"

"Yes..." came hesitantly from the direction where Kollerup assumed the bar was.

"Do you have any flashlights?"

"We do!"

"Do you have one on you?"

"No, but there are some at the front desk."

"Does anyone here have their phones with them?"

Suddenly, several pale lights glowed to life around the room. People could see a little once more, but Kolle still thought it could get even brighter.

"What about the tablets? The displays on those things give off more light. Turn off your phones, and save your batteries!"

Darkness engulfed them once more, but only for a moment, at which point several people at the bar activated the tablets at that station.

"Bring two of those things over here," Kollerup ordered. The pale lights shakily made their way over to him. "Anybody hurt?" he asked the crowd at large.

"I banged my knee," someone complained meekly.

"Anything else?" Bumped his knee! Clearly a sign of the end times, Kolle thought.

"Is the child all right?" he now wanted to know.

The mother responded, "Nothing happened. Everything's fine."

"Nobody leaves the room." He added a please to this, because his talking shower tought him a lesson. "As soon as we get the situation under control, you'll be allowed to go to your rooms, but it's safest here for now."

Outside, the storm could be heard whistling around as sheets of water from the rain clouds pelted the building and its windows.

"Kolle!" echoed from the entrance. Onne!

"Onne!" Kolle was glad to see the little chap.

"The sheep are fine!" shouted the shepherd.

"What's going on, Onne? Do you know more than we do?"

"Lightning must've struck the generator shed," he said.

"We should go see if we can still salvage it, Onne." Kolle pointed toward the terrace.

Just then, two employees showed up with flashlights. Kolle took one, and he passed two more to Onne and the hotel manager.

"Here's the deal: your employees should stay here with the guests. Someone should tend to the injured and take care of any cuts or bruises. Coffee and tea wouldn't be bad right about now." General murmurs rose. Chairs and tables were back upright. The kitchen staff got to work in the kitchen, and somehow normalcy returned.

Since the entrance as well as the foyer were on the leeward side, Kolle took his chances and cautiously opened the door.

He knew that on that side of a building, the suction that storms could generate wasn't inconsiderable. Most roof damage from detaching roof tiles occurred on the downwind side. The suction was comparable to the effect that caused an airplane to gain lift above its wings.

"Uh," Onne hesitated.

"What?" Kolle glanced at him.

"I hope you're not afraid of water. You'll be drenched in no time," Onne said with an innocent twinkle in his eye.

"Do I look like I'm made out of sugar?" asked Kolle.

"I'm just saying." That settled the matter.

Two minutes later, Kolle found himself wishing for a rain coat. But in this weather, it didn't matter whether you were outside with one on or not, because the storm, which had now become a hurricane, was driving the rain horizontally in front of it. On this particular night, hell was a night-black wall of rain. With a broad, rolling gait like real sailors on a pitching ship, they staggered to the terrace and braced themselves against the storm. It was pitch dark, and all they had were the quivering beams of light from their two flashlights to guide their way. They could just as easily have been in a black wind tunnel. Kolle sensed it coming before they crept around the next corner. Instinctively, he yanked Onne to the ground, and something large flew over their heads with a flapping sound.

"That was close!" Onne roared in Kolle's ear. They scrambled on their hands and knees to the terrace. There lay the dead man... or at least Kolle assumed the man was dead.

Face up; eyes and mouth open. No pulse, no breath. At least fifteen minutes had passed since the man had collapsed at the terrace door. The hue of the man's skin and Kolle's intuition, combined with a nonexistent pulse, all validated his suspicion. He looked toward the terrace window and, with a shrug, indicated to the bystanders in the restaurant that there was nothing more to be done.

"Let's get him inside!" He nodded to Onne, and they both lifted the heavy, limp body.

Lightning darted out from the departing storm, and the hurricane subsided a bit, although it was still blowing so hard that they both moved cautiously to avoid being struck by flying objects. It didn't matter that they were moving so slowly, though, since they were saturated by now anyway; as if they had showered with their clothes on. Kolle was gradually getting chilly too. The temperature had dropped at least ten degrees, or so it seemed to him. When they got to the leeward side, the noise around them suddenly went down. A hurricane? Kolle wondered. He gazed up at the sky, where the stars were twinkling down out of a huge hole in the sky. Dripping wet, Kolle and Onne trudged into the building and carried the dead man through the restaurant.

"We don't have much time!" he shouted to the crowd. "Where's the refrigerator?"

"This way! On the other side of the kitchen." The manager's face was now as pale as snow. "Why, that's Wolters!" he called out.

"Who's Wolters?" Kollerup glanced at him sharply.

"Our mudflat guide!"

"Ex-mudflat guide, you mean."

"Yes. He was supposed to lead a mudflat hike today, but it didn't happen in the end."

"Then what was he still doing here?"

"By the time he was done complaining to my wife, it was too late for him to safely walk back through the mudflats. In those instances, we have an extra room available in the staff lodge, so he spends the night."

"Never mind. Off to the fridge with him!"

The three of them carried the body into the cold storage area and deposited it on a table.

"Let's get out of here!" Kollerup was frozen to the bone. Onne went on to answer the questions of the guests in the restaurant. A hurricane! They all knew about those from TV, but here? On the North Sea? Waterspouts, sure; they were common enough, as were the tornadoes that had recently started to materialize around here, the ones that caused huge masses of water to rise to great heights out at sea. But maybe this was just a windstorm. You could never say for sure about the capricious weather these days.

"Is the net working right now, Onne?"

"No, it isn't," the hotel manager beat him to it.

"Shit." Kolle considered his options.

He turned to the manager. "What about satellite connectivity?"

"It isn't autonomous; it's hooked up to the power grid. Who'd expect a lightning strike like that to shut everything down, either?" It almost seemed as if the manager felt responsible for the blackout. "The only thing we have left is gas for the kitchen," he said.

"I need a list of the guests." Kolle silently prayed that there was such a list, but when he saw the manager's face, his hope sank.

"But Nele can tell you who has checked in. Wait." He turned to the restaurant and called out, "Nele! Come over here, please." The slender Nordic beauty with the blond pageboy approached.

"Yes?" Big brown eyes gazed at her boss.

"Tell the inspector the names of the guests who checked in, please."

And with that, she instantly began to rattle off the names of all the guests.

"Wait a minute, wait a minute!" laughed Kolle, before asking Onne to jot down the names. He acquired a tablet and a stylus, and it took a second for him to pull up the app.

"Well," Kolle glanced at Nele. When she was done, she earned an array of admiring looks.

"Photographic memory," the manager declared, moved. "Nele is worth her weight in gold."

"I'm sure that's helpful in your line of work," Kolle said dryly. The woman in question seemed unmoved by this remark.

"It ends up being a curse sometimes. I can't forget anything quickly," she said, and something seemed to make her suddenly sad.

There were ten rooms in the hotel in all: six upstairs and four downstairs. Four were occupied upstairs, and two downstairs. Kolle thanked Nele and the manager for their help.

"Oh yes—" he remembered something. "Who actually takes care of the building services?"

"Jan-Ole," the hotel manager replied. "Should I tell him to take a look at the damage?"

"Yes. Good idea!" Kolle nodded with satisfaction. "What about the connection to the mainland?" he wanted to know.

"We'll have to see when the power comes back. Anyway, the landline is dead, but when the power from the mainland is restored, we'll know when the satellite is back." The manager stared outside and added dryly, "But considering those tall, thick clouds, it doesn't look so good."

"Let's hope and pray," Kolle muttered. "Send someone to take a look at the upper floors. I need to take a shower and put on something dry. And he does too." He pointed to Onne, who was now sitting on a chair wrapped in a blanket and sipping something hot. The manager gave a wave, and a young fellow trotted off. After fifteen minutes, he returned.

"All clear upstairs. The windows are fine, and the roof seems undamaged. That's bordering on a miracle, chief." All the manager said in reply was, "We spent a ton of money storm-proofing the place." For him, that seemed to be the end of the matter.

Kolle didn't care. As the winds picked up again outside, he was happy to still have hot water for his shower, although there were no comments this time from Betty.

As he searched for his clothes in the glow of the flashlight, the lights came back on, but went out again after a flicker. Then the power flashed back on again. Kolle waited a bit before turning off his flashlight. When he still had light after two minutes, he breathed a sigh of relief.

In the hallway, Kolle ran into Onne, who was just leaving one of the unoccupied rooms. The pants he had been given were cuffed several times, and the sweatshirt, which was much too big, bagged around his torso.

"Not a single word!" he rebuked Kolle threateningly with a shake of his finger.

"I wouldn't dream of saying anything, though I did wonder what your borrowed underwear must look like."

"What underwear?" Onne shot back.

They both had a good laugh at this. Back at the bar, the first thing Kolle ordered was two triple whiskeys, Irish ones this time, neat.

To the manager, who was standing in the kitchen going over the grocery lists with the chef, he called, "You can send the guests up to their rooms, so they can try to get a good night's sleep. No one's escaping in this weather, but lock all the doors just in case. And have your employees stay inside too, please. No one should leave this swaying ship." After a brief pause, Kolle added, "Any word from your technician?"

The hotel manager seemed relieved as he said, "Yes. He just checked in on his radio. It looks bad, but he thinks he can make some temporary repairs."

As Kolle and Onne sat in the deep club chairs, the detective lit two cigarettes, which were stuffed with a special blend. We've earned this, Kolle thought as he offered Onne one of the joints. After cocking one eyebrow, Onne accepted the offer. Ensconced in their comfortable lounge chairs with soft muzak filling the air, they kept each other company for a while, chuckling and drinking; the bartender had been kind enough to put the bottle on the bar. They didn't stop at one joint either. Hours later, they dozed off to the sounds of ACDC's "Whole Lotta Rosie." A cheesy piano lounge version, of course.

"Thank God Angus didn't learn to play the piano back then, just the guitar," Onne remarked drowsily.

HOTEL
First day after the storm
8:00 a.m.

THE NEXT DAY DAWNED EXACTLY LIKE OUR TWO heroes in the bar—gray and cloudy. Someone had changed the music.

"It's supposed to be encouraging," groaned Kollerup. This musical drivel was doing nothing for him. He dragged himself to the reception desk.

He pulled himself up to the counter, slurring his words with a heavy tongue. "Hello! Anyone there?"

Maik stepped out of the office.

"Moin, Inspector!" he greeted Kollerup.

"Sssh!" Kolle hissed with his index finger over his mouth. "Not so loud!"

Apologizing, Maik raised both his hands and said a little more quietly, "What can I do for you?"

"You can tell me what it'll take to hear some normal music around here."

"Normal?"

"Yes, normal music. Rock music, made by humans. Normal, like every normal person listens to."

"Rock music?"

"Yes."

"One second." He went into the office. "Like ACDC or something similar?" he yelled.

"Not this morning! Something out of the sixties or seventies."

"Pink Floyd?"

Kolle sighed, relieved. "Yes!"

Seconds later, the first notes from "Shine On You Crazy Diamond" rang out.

"You have saved my life, Maik!"

"From my personal collection, the Pink Floyd CD Box."

Back in the restaurant, it smelled like coffee. Kollerup crept up cautiously to the sideboard where breakfast was being prepared and sniffed the coffee pot. I knew it, he triumphed inwardly. The last blast of the blackest roast. Onne was slurping on a cup, sucking down the tarry stuff.

"If I look as beat up as you do, we'd be perfect in a zombie film!" he greeted his new friend.

"Yeah, sure, and we could smear this black stuff on our faces. It would be as scary as hell."

Kolle wanted some normal drip coffee, which he ordered from Nele, who looked like she had spent the night at a beauty spa. He took a seat. As soon as he had his coffee, Budnik, the hotel manager, materialized.

"Good morning, Inspector. Bad news. The power supply from the mainland, the landline and satellite connections are all down."

"Have you already been outside?"

"Yes, the jetty is totally destroyed. No ship can dock here for the next few days."

"That's good. Then no one can escape." Kolle was happy.

"It's high tide right now anyway," Budnik said. Kolle nodded and gratefully sipped his regular cup of coffee.

"However," the hotel manager raised his finger, "we have radio reception."

"That's great!"

"But it doesn't look good on the mainland. Several smaller vessels were reported to have been washed ashore; houses with no roofs, uprooted trees. No deaths, thank goodness, but several hundred people were injured. The Technical Relief Service and the German army are working on clean up. There won't be any ferry service until tomorrow morning. The islands got off lightly. How it looks on the other halligs is unknown.

Kolle thought.

"Helicopter!" he called out, voicing his idea.

"They say they're all being used. The news and the special broadcasts are reporting that all those available are in the air, helping with the clean-up efforts. As for the halligs and the islands, they're asking us to hold out for one more day."

"So, that's the status? Alright." He glanced at his watch. "I would like to examine the dead man. My limited knowledge will have to suffice at this time. I'll start with the first interviews at eleven. Please make sure the guests are available then. But right now, I need to eat something."

After breakfast, he went outside with Onne. The cool air hit him. There wasn't much to see on the Wadden Sea, though. Thick fog limited their visibility to no more than twenty meters.

"It's 64," said Onne, looking at the outside thermometer. What they could see at first glance presented nothing unusual, but then they strolled along the garden path and had to dodge several battered pieces of trees.

"Trees!" Kolle exclaimed in amazement.

"Yes, probably from the mainland or from Hooge over there. Only the vultures know exactly," replied Onne.

There was nothing left of the jetty. The finest tropical wood and oak logs, simply gone. Then they headed toward the chapel; Onne was quite worried about what they would find.

As they walked up, the first sheep were scrambling free, and Onne counted them quickly. There were just as many as before: exactly two hundred rams. The artsy shepherd exhaled. His hut was the only thing that had been damaged. The roof was gone, and all the window panes were destroyed.

"We can repair it!" Onne exclaimed cheerfully.

The inside of the hut looked like it had been through an

earthquake; not one single picture still hung on the walls. Kolle was horrified! All of Onne's work, his paintings, wiped out just like that. But his friend seemed to be in good spirits. Whistling a song, he poked around his former home. He lifted one thing after the other, exclaiming as he did so, "Everything can be fixed." Then he went into the corner where the wash area was. It was still intact, and the door of the shower was latched shut. With a theatrical "Aha!," Onne ripped the door open. There they lay! His pictures, carefully lashed in a tarp. "We'll need to carry everything up to the hotel later, but for now, they can remain here." Onne deliberately relatched the door of the shower and then they continued their examination of the hut.

"Tell me, what do you think about last night?" Kollerup asked.

Onne was searching for his refrigerator in the rubble, and Kollerup realized that the painter hadn't heard his question.

"What are you doing?"

"Beer. I'm looking for my beer."

"Forget your crappy beer! There's nothing left here!"

"No, they can't be gone."

"It's just normal beer! They have the same brand up at the hotel."

"No."

"What do you mean, no?"

"They don't have this kind in the hotel. I'd be rather surprised."

"There it is! Give me a hand."

Kolle groaned but helped anyway.

"Aha!" Onne held up two brown bottles triumphantly. Not exactly impressive, Kolle thought. They looked nothing like beer bottles, but rather like old wine bottles, the necks sealed with red wax.

"Do you know what that is?" Onne waved it under Kolle's nose.

"Beer?"

"Yeah, sure! But what kind of beer?"

"Flensburger?"

"I doubt they had anything to do with these."

"You don't mean to say you drink beer from our rivals, the Dithmarschers!"

"Oh, no!" Onne was as happy as Rumpelstilskin.

"Okay, I give up." Kolle had run out of patience for this game.

"It is the oldest beer that you can have around here." Onne loved his riddles. He started rummaging around again, and found some reasonably dry newspaper under a woodpile. He wrapped the bottles in this carefully and handed one of them to Kollerup.

"Don't drop it," he warned him.

"Don't drink it would be a more appropriate warning right now," grinned Kollerup.

They walked back to the hotel in silence. Kolle could wait. When Onne was ready, he would pour him a glass of this pure wine, or, as it was, pure beer. As far as they could see, the other structures and the hotel seemed to have survived the hurricane unscathed.

The salt marshes themselves, of course, no longer looked as idyllic as before. Flotsam of all sizes and types lay around, including some corrugated iron roofing pieces, probably from a shed on a neighboring hallig. A large piece was stuck diagonally in the grass like a crashed spaceship. Otherwise, they could see everything that one usually finds after a storm surge: plastic bottles, boxes, beams, and canisters. And also a stroller, which gave Kolle pause. He hoped that the child's mother had managed to get them both to safety before the storm hit.

"Tell me, do you hear that?"

He stood still and listened. "No. I don't hear anything."

"That's what I mean!"

"This quiet?"

"Yeah!"

No wind, no seagulls; even the water, somewhere out there in the fog, was completely silent. No signal horns from ships. Even the usual humming of ships' engines, hardly perceptible in calm weather like this, was missing. It was dead silent.

HALLIG
Three days before the storm
Noon

RELENTLESS HEAT AND HUMIDITY, RIVALING THAT in tropical latitudes, struck the retired Sieverstens as the passengers exited the air conditioning of the ferry and stepped onto the hallig.

Somewhat lost, they stood on the jetty, at first uncertain about what they should do next. Shouldn't the hotel send a car to pick them up? The friendly ferry staff had carried their luggage—four suitcases and two bags-- to the pier. They looked at each other, perplexed.

"We could take two suitcases to the hotel," suggested Kurt Sieversten.

Heidi Sieversten didn't seem to like this suggestion at all. "No. We paid," she replied resolutely and added, "And baggage transport is part of the service!"

"Look!" Kurt pointed at the hotel dwelling mound that, along with the massive structure of the haubarg, dominated the hallig. The freshly whitewashed walls shone brilliantly against the blue summer sky, decorated with the little blue clouds that would make any picture postcard photographer cheer with joy. A small car moved silently toward them, winding its way down the curving one-way road toward the jetty. A young man jumped out of the electric vehicle with a "Moin!"

"Moin!" replied Kurt and Heidi in chorus.

"I'm Knut. Welcome to Grienoog!"

With a firm handshake, he greeted them both and asked them to take a seat in the car. After he'd stowed the luggage, they glided silently to the hotel.

"Your first time on Grienoog?" Nonchalantly, one hand on the steering wheel, Knut turned toward the back.

"Yeah," replied Kurt. Heidi, who was suffering from the heat, said nothing.

"Then you will certainly enjoy your stay." Their driver pointed to a church and said, "That back there is our main attraction. The chapel is more than three hundred years old. In front of it is our next highlight: our sheep." About eighty sheep were panting and ruminating on a large meadow in front of the chapel, which stood on a mound like every building there.

Somewhat off to the side stood a small hut, in front of which a little person in an undershirt was sitting at an easel, smearing a canvas with dark paint.

"Onne," explained the young man. "Our shepherd-painter, and the third attraction here on Grienoog."

As they drove up the driveway to the entrance of the hotel, it was almost as if they were flying. They rocked to a gentle, full stop, and Knut helped them get out.

In the foyer they were greeted by a Frisian beauty. "Moin, I'm Nele. Welcome to Grienoog! If you'd please come this way to reception? Knut will take care of your luggage."

When they had completed the formalities, each was handed a beeper.

"With this, you can call for the electric vehicle at any time, and Knut will pick you up."

Initially Kurt wanted to refuse to take it.

"On a hallig? You can comfortably walk..." but Heidi nudged him in the side and took both beepers. Svenja, the receptionist, smiled and explained to them the usual breakfast times and the amenities that guests could enjoy here. "Also, you can use the e-bikes. Free of charge for hotel guests."

In the room, the couple marveled at the technological novelties of sanitary engineering. A talking shower! However, it took them a little while to get used to the fact that there was no faucet in the sink. Photocells controlled the water supply and the temperature. And the toilet was self-cleaning. In the sleeping area, they had access to a TV that provided news from around the world and a tablet they could use to surf the internet or read their daily newspapers.

Before dinner, they had plenty of time to explore the hallig, and so they decided to try out the e-bikes. Neither was terribly athletic, but why not try them out if they were free? In light summer clothing, they swung onto the bikes and cycled off on the circular route. The meadows were covered with blooming flowers at this time of year. Next to the early blooms of the purple beach lilac, the bright wormwood looks quite delightful, thought Heidi Siervertsen.

At the sheep pasture, they paused and watched the diminutive painter, who was still busy with his canvas. When he noticed them, he looked over and waved his brush at them in a friendly manner.

"Moin!" he hollered at them.

They waved back and headed for the chapel. Unfortunately, the entrance was blocked by a low fence, and it took some effort for them to take a look inside. From a distance, the building looked much larger than it really was. The chapel was more like a small cottage than a former house of worship. It had a small bell tower, around which swifts were circling at breakneck speed, but otherwise the building looked shabby. The roof of the structure was caulked, and some of the windows were provisionally nailed shut with wooden slats. The entrance on the west side, a yawning hole, was poorly protected from the dire weather conditions by its corrugated metal fence. From their vantage point at the fence, several sheep watched the two humans with interest. Others lay panting beside a water trough in the shadow of the tower.

Then Heidi and Kurt rode past an extremely well-manicured patch of lawn with a large H of yellow flagstones in the middle. A helipad! They had thought of everything on this hallig.

A large residential house stood beside the square, up on a mound like every building on the halligs. Adjacent to the helipad was a rather large miniature golf course. Next to it stood a hut, which was locked. A sign above the door informed them that the facility belonged to the hotel, and next to it, the opening hours were posted. Between the hours of 9 a.m. to 2 p.m. and 3 p.m. to 8 p.m., you could hurl small balls into the salt marshes. Then they passed the pier and continued along the circular path to the hotel beach.

This was also surprisingly large, stretching southward from the eastern side of the hallig to directly below the hotel. Several beach chairs were generously distributed across the sand, all with good views of the Wadden Sea. Boardwalks made from the finest tropical wood connected the mound with the beach bar where they would dine today.

The entire time they were on the road, Kurt and Heidi spoke very little. They didn't say anything, except for an occasional "Look at that," or a "Is that Amrum back there?"

Kurt took pictures with his phone from time to time, and Heidi limited herself to instructing him on what he should take pictures of. After all, they weren't here for pleasure, even if their stay vaguely resembled a Caribbean vacation.

Back in their room, they saved the photos on their laptop and closely studied them. When the chapel appeared on the monitor, they were in silent agreement. This was where they would get their revenge. The church was ideal.

They were not alone when they came down for dinner. At

the next table sat a family with a very well-behaved boy who, quite uncharacteristically for a child his age, sat absolutely still as he chatted with his mother. His hair was freshly combed, and designer glasses were perched on his nose. He was wearing a Hawaiian shirt that still showed the creases from the store.

Poor lad, how old could he be? Five, maybe six, thought Kurt Sievertsen.

He glanced at his wife, who obviously had the same thing going through her mind, and smiled. Their daughter had been quite different at that age. Hardly tamable. She had always had a question ready, an indication of her infinite interest in the world.

The boy's parents looked quite at home in the hotel's modern ambiance. On the other hand, this was not Kurt's world. He and Heidi could easily afford it, but thinking back to how things had been in the seventies, he felt that less had been better. No flat screen in every room.

The latest news from around the world was running constantly in the foyer, at the bar, and also on the wall of the restaurant bar. In the past, you went on vacation, and that was that. No TV, maybe the radio in the background, and at most the local daily newspaper in the evening. As for decor, Kurt didn't mind used furniture if it was really old, but the new vintage-looking stuff got on his nerves. It smelled and felt new, but looked like Grandpa's summer house. Painted light gray, with an emphasis on "painted," because every brush hair had left a white-gray trace in the "rustic look" of the furniture. Then the furniture makers had sanded it down and added another layer, a shade darker, and they had done this over and over again until four coats of paint were visible. Better the sticky counter of his old village pub with its dark-brown wooden stools, one of which always wobbled, passed wistfully through Kurt's mind.

The man, about forty years old, was talking on his phone; fragments of sentences floated over to them.

"Yes... Maybach here. What do you mean, tomorrow doesn't work... ah... yes, well, then next Sunday... Good, still before the mudflat tour... yes, alright. No problem. See you then, Mr. Wolters." Setting aside his phone, Maybach ordered the waitress over with a snap of his fingers. Kurt snorted disdainfully. Entitled jerk. He smiled at his wife. She had heard the name too.

A slim woman entered the restaurant. She looked to be past fifty, but Kurt guessed that in her youth she must have turned all the men's heads. Short gray hair, darker complexion. She looked around uncertainly and took a seat next to the open patio door, overlooking the sea.

Kurt's wife seemed to be lost in thought. He touched her hand, and she returned to reality. He leaned forward and whispered, "Soon it will be over." She nodded as she ate the rest of her dessert.

"Well then," he said out loud. They both stood up, left the restaurant through the patio door, and strolled down to the beach. A beautiful sunset. Nevertheless, it was still infernally hot, and the light breeze did nothing to cool them down. Small waves sloshed lazily on the artificial beach.

They ordered mixed drinks at the beach bar and sat down in two of the beach chairs. For a while, they let their thoughts wander. Then Heidi Sievertsen pulled her camera out of her shoulder bag, and they looked at the pictures they had taken on their hallig bike tour. Yes, absolutely. The old chapel was ideal. That's where they would lure him and then punish him.

They were on the hallig to bring justice to the man responsible for their daughter's death.

HALLIG
First day after the storm
9 a.m.

KOLLE AND ONNE JUST STOOD THERE, SIMPLY LISTENING for a while. Then when Onne grew bored, he nudged Kolle and asked him to go to the hotel. The Husum inspector was suddenly very thoughtful.

"I don't know…" Kollerup sighed and shook his head.

"What do you not know?"

"Well, think about it. We're here on a piece of land that once was part of the mainland. A hallig."

"Yeah, and?" Onne looked at his friend.

"Many towns and villages met their end as the result of high storm-surges. It probably had something to do with global warming and its consequences."

"Well…" Onne shook his head.

"Well, what?"

Onne raised a finger. "After the great ice age, when the mammoths disappeared and people moved north again in increasing numbers, the temperature kept going up. That couldn't have been the cause of man-made climate change."

"Yes, I know." Kolle also knew that there had been a continuous cooling and warming over the previous centuries.

"But what I want to say is that we now seem to be living in a warming period again. However, this warming is being felt all over the earth, and it's happening faster than the last warming periods in the earth's history. The recent storm, which may have been a hurricane, is one such sign."

Onne shook his head skeptically. "Maybe so, but was it really a hurricane?" He shrugged. "Look," he said and stopped. "Even if it was, what are you going to do about it?"

"Nothing. I just thought it was significant that we're once again living in a time of warming and rising storm surges. And we are witnessing the consequences of rising sea levels." He stomped one foot. "On this hallig."

"Well, everything ebbs and flows." Onne was the more pragmatic on that point. "Nothing stays the same."

"Speaking of flowing—" Kolle lifted a beer bottle wrapped in newspaper. "Is this drinkable?"

"Nothing stays the same," Onne repeated with a grin.

At the hotel, they got to work. First up, an examination of the corpse, and then, time to question the suspects. It didn't look like help would be coming from the mainland any time soon, so Kollerup had to improvise as best as he could. He borrowed a digital camera and a tripod from Jan-Ole, the hotel technician, and a box of disposable gloves from the kitchen. Today, he would have to do without the obligatory lab suit.

First, he had the deceased moved from the cold room to a downstairs room. Wolters was no lightweight. Onne, Maybach and he had quite a bit of trouble hoisting the body onto the improvised operating table. Forbidding any disturbance, he set up the camera and began a cursory examination of the dead man.

"Time of death is known." Kollerup noted the time and glanced at Onne, who just shrugged.

"All the guests saw him die."

"Exactly, Onne," confirmed Kolle.

"We'll need to examine the dead man for external wounds and such now, won't we?" Onne seemed to be quite excited about this. "Cool. Just like on TV."

"Yep."

"Magnifying glass?"

"Yep!"

"Here!"

For the next few minutes, it was so quiet in the room that you could hear the sheep bleating in the meadow. Onne picked up the camera and recorded Kolle, who announced the current time, who was present, and who was to be examined.

"I am beginning with the feet. On the soles of the feet..." he sniffed them and continued, "sheep droppings."

"Not unusual for this hallig," Onne muttered and zoomed in on the sole with the feces.

"Clothing." Kolle continued his study of the corpse. "Light summer clothing. Pants, lightweight shirt. Undamaged. Forearms show abrasions. Ante mortem."

"Huh?"

Kollerup rolled his eyes. "Because the abrasions are scabbed over. Once you die, the blood stops flowing."

"Oh, right," Onne apologized meekly.

"Next. The pants are heavily soiled at the knees. In addition, the palms of the hands are injured."

"Also ante?"

"What's that?"

"Before death, or after death, or the cause of death?" Onne stared at him, smiling.

"If you keep asking questions, you'll get an ante-mortem black eye." Kolle grinned back and waved the magnifying glass menacingly. "Face and head, no injury. But—" he now came to the essential and obvious matter, "on the neck, there is a cut about four inches long. An irregular, wavy edge. And there's something in the wound."

While Onne intensely examined the wound, Kollerup strode over to the door, tore it open, and collided with the technician. "A needle-nosed pliers, please. Quickly."

Jan-Ole ran off. The hotel manager watched him go. "Discover something yet?"

"No." Kolle remembered. "Oh, yes, please tell everyone that I will start the interviews in about an hour."

"Of course, Inspector."

Jan-Ole returned with a pair of pliers. Kollerup grabbed them and closed the door, before carefully probing the wound. He then held an elongated object up for the camera.

"Hey, not so fast, or it'll be blurred." Onne zoomed back a bit until the image was sharp on the display.

"Looks like a piece of corrugated metal. About four inches long and two inches wide," declared Kolle. Glancing around, he realized he had no plastic bags, so he called for the hotel manager, who shortly afterward stuck his head into the room.

"I need some plastic bags!" Kollerup exclaimed, angry with himself. Less than a minute later, he had a whole box of ziploc bags. Carefully he bagged the evidence, all under the sharp eye of the camera.

He raised an index finger and pointed at the bag, speaking into the lens like a television host. "So, the first preliminary result: shortly before his death, the man, being still alive at the time, sustained abrasions on his hands, arms and knees, probably as the result of a fall. In his neck, on the right side, is a wound in which the piece of corrugated iron just shown was stuck. Around the otherwise clean wound, no crust of dried blood. I will now undress the dead man."

Followed by the camera, he stepped to the door with a muttered curse and asked the hotel manager for several garbage bags. One by one, he bagged the clothes after he examined them for visible evidence. When the body lay naked in front of him, he asked Onne to attach the camera to a tripod. Together they flipped the corpse onto its stomach. No lividity. Kollerup spoke loudly so the recording would be clear enough. "The body shows no evidence of hypostasis. This means that there was not enough, if any, blood in the body to cause the typical discolorations after his death."

They turned the body on its back again. Now Kolle thoroughly examined the skin for injuries. An unpleasant procedure, since Kolle had never liked getting up close with corpses; after all, he was a police officer, not a doctor or a forensic scientist. But he managed to get the job firmly behind him. Once he felt that there was nothing else for them to find, he wrapped the body in trash bags and taped it up like a package. The clothing, the piece of corrugated iron, and the corpse itself all went back into the walk-in refrigerator. The memory card from the camera also went into a bag, which landed in Kollerup's pocket. Better safe than sorry, he thought. He then realized he was hungry.

In the restaurant, the tables were set for lunch. The hotel manager had decided that everyone should eat at a single table; after all, they were trapped here together. No one protested.

The guests were all subdued. Only the six-year-old Malte, the Maybachs' son, talked a blue streak. Everything was a great adventure to him. Even when the dead man had been carried past him last night, he had seemed more excited than anxious.

A tense conversation only slowly gained steam among the guests. How long would it take for their Gilligan's Island experience to end? How were their friends and relatives on the mainland? How extensive was the storm damage? The questions circled the group, but no one had a satisfactory answer. The radio broadcasters repeatedly said the damage was substantial, and the number of injuries was altered with each passing hour. The population was asked to refrain from traveling anywhere by car. Electricity had been restored in almost all municipalities, but since the disaster had hit, there were more rescue vehicles on the road than private vehicles. The newscaster kept repeating the famous English slogan from World War II over and over again: "Keep calm and carry on."

When the first guests seemed to be done eating, Kollerup cleared his throat loudly and stood up. Such attention embarrassed him, and he didn't quite know where to start.

"Some of you presumably still don't know who I am. My name is Kollerup, and I am the Chief Inspector of the Husum Murder Squad. I'm actually here on vacation, but unfortunately things have turned out a little differently." Kolle was searching for the right words. "Anyway, you know our situation: a man has died before our eyes. My task now is to find the cause of death, to secure evidence, and interrogate witnesses. Since you know that we are stuck here at the moment, I'm asking for your help."

Kollerup watched the reactions of the guests while he was speaking. "So, I will talk with all of you today. Please try to remember the day and the hours before the storm hit. Did you notice anything? What seemed strange to you? The more you tell me the better. I don't care how unimportant it seems to you." He glanced around. After a brief pause, he added, "Anything could be important."

Onne murmured that he was very proud of Kolle, but he still needed to tell the guests how he wanted to proceed. Kollerup sat down and ordered a coffee. By the time he realized he'd forgotten to be specific, a cup of the best drip coffee around was already in front of him. He smiled gratefully at Nele. After taking a deep sip, he stood back up.

"Everyone, one more thing."

Nobody had expected this, and the room grew dead silent.

"Since the weather is relatively calm now, I can certainly understand that you might like to go outside. However, I still have to follow the usual procedures." He then listed the names of the guests and asked them to come to the office at the reception desk at thirty-minute intervals in the order he had just read their names.

HOTEL
First day after the storm
2 p.m.

CHRISTA HANSEN WAS THE FIRST GUEST TO BE interviewed. A slender, attractive woman whose true age was difficult to determine, though she had certainly passed the half-century mark as her hands and gray hair revealed. Kolle had a knack for guessing someone's age from their hands. Her neck showed only a few wrinkles, but her face bore scattered lines that came more from laughing than worry. From what he could see, she didn't have an extra ounce of fat on her body, and everything was in its original place. She seemed to have spent a lot of time in the sun recently. Her tan looked natural, not like the sort you got in a tanning salon. He couldn't call her a classic beauty—her nose was a tad too crooked for that, and her eyes a bit too far apart—but in her youth, she must have broken many a man's heart.

He skipped the welcoming handshake and asked her to take a seat with a wave of his hand. After offering her something to drink, he started the audio recording on a borrowed tablet.

"Would you tell me your full name? Clearly please." Kolle pointed to the device.

"Christa Hansen."

"Where is your current place of residence?"

"I live in Hamburg, Ottostraße 17."

"What do you do for a living?"

"I work as a freelance consultant for a US company that builds wind turbines."

"A freelance consultant?"

"Yes, ever since I retired a year ago. Since my pension isn't enough to live on, I continue to work on a contract basis."

"Why are you here on the hallig?"

"To meet with Mr. Maybach." When she saw the knowing look on the policeman's face, she swiftly added, "For business."

"What was there to discuss?"

"It has nothing to do with the case," she replied snappishly.

"I need to decide that for myself."

She hesitated briefly. "All right." After a moment, she continued. "Mr. Maybach has found a way to increase the efficiency of wind turbines by almost eighty percent."

"Really?" Kolle looked at her questioningly.

"This is an enormous step forward. At the moment the average efficiency is fifty percent. Even vertical—" She interrupted herself because she noticed that he obviously had no idea what she was talking about. "So, what we have here on the coast are horizontal turbines. The axis of rotation is horizontal. But there are also those turbines whose axis of rotation is vertical. These are the vertical turbines."

"I see."

"Yes, and the vertical turbines have a maximum efficiency of forty percent."

"What has Maybach invented?"

"A way to increase this to almost eighty percent for the vertical turbines. You understand what that means?"

"No, what does it mean?"

"No?" She gazed at the policeman in amazement. "Isn't it obvious?" She sighed and continued. "Do you know of even one vertical plant here on the coast? No, right? The industry has committed itself to horizontal turbines. Worldwide, almost ninety percent of the installations are built this way. A breakthrough invention in vertical turbines would result in a huge increase in profits in the traditional wind industry."

"So you, as the representative of this US company, have been asked to purchase the rights to this invention from Maybach?"

"Correct."

"And you were able to buy the patent or whatever from him?"

"No. You have to do something like that carefully. My plan was to discuss the concrete details with him next week. He wasn't opposed to this suggestion, but he wanted a few more days to think things over."

"Ah, okay..." Kolle tapped a thoughtful finger on the table and asked casually, "Did you know the dead man before now?"

"Yes."

"Ah."

"I had a relationship with him years ago."

"Did you know that Wolters lived here?"

"No, I didn't know that, but I did know he came from Föhr."

"How and where did you meet?"

"Forty years ago, in Hamburg. He was studying mechanical engineering, and I had enrolled in business administration."

"How long did your relationship last?"

"Until he graduated, so almost five years. Then he moved to the States. We wrote a few times, but then lost touch with each other." She shrugged with regret.

"It must have been sad for you." Kollerup studied her sympathetically.

"Oh, no." Now she was playing it cool. "There were enough other applicants," she said—somewhat snippily, Kolle thought.

"After that, you never heard from him again?"

"No."

"So, you did?"

"No, we had no further contact." She remained quite calm, but the skin around her nose grew a little paler.

"Good. Then please send—" he looked at his notes, but then mumbled: "Could it be that Wolters was also after this invention?"

Christa Hansen suddenly stood up stiffly, clearly wishing to ignore this question. "That is beyond my knowledge," she answered flaty.

"Well, then..." Kolle now stood up as well. "That's it for now. If I need anything else, I know where to find you." He noticed as he passed her and held the door open for her, that the cool lady had fine beads of perspiration on her forehead. Without much thought, he suddenly called after her: "Where were you yesterday between nine and nine-thirty?"

She stopped, seeming to think.

"At dinner. I had just placed my order when Wolters collapsed at the window. Is that all?"

"Yes, thanks."

FERRY
Six days before the storm
6 p.m.

"Malte!" Marianne Maybach plucked her son from the rail of the Sandcrab, her grip enhanced by years of strength training. "Malte, please, you know that I already told you several times not to climb on the ship's handrail!" She especially emphasized the word please.

"It's called a railing, Mom!"

"It doesn't matter. You are not to go over there again! Do we understand each other? Stay close to me. Do you want the sharks to eat you?"

"Mom," he rolled his eyes, "cat sharks don't eat kids." He had read that in a book somewhere, and his mother sighed. What else could you teach a gifted six-year-old? He didn't get his brains from her, she thought as she called over to her husband. "Frank! Could you please"—and she stressed the please again—"tell your son not to do that?"

Frank Maybach glanced at his wife and smiled. They were both practically the same age, to the day. It was obvious to others that keeping fit through sports and taking care of their health were important to him and his wife. Their clothing also distinguished them from the average passenger. It was easy to see they were doing well financially. Of course both of them wanted only the best for their son, and he sometimes let Malte get away with one thing or another. He squinted at the sun and called his son. "Malte!" He raised his voice a little on the second syllable as if he were going to ask a question.

"Yes, Dad?"

"Malte, you remember what I said?"

"Yes. I should behave."

"Good, then behave. We don't want to scare your mother, do we?"

"Yes, Dad. No!"

"In complete sentences, please."

"Yes, Dad. We don't want to scare Mom."

"Alright. Now go and buy yourself an ice cream, but please go slowly."

"Yes, Dad. I will buy myself an ice cream slowly."

Malte strolled slowly into the passenger area, but as soon as he was out of his parents' sight, he started zooming down the aisle like an airplane with his arms outstretched. He slammed two euros down on the counter and said in a deep voice, "A rum and coke ice cream, please."

The seller's eyes widened. "My boy…" However, he was interrupted by Malta's deep voice, "Make it fast! It's an emergency!"

The man behind the counter chuckled. "I'm not allowed to sell you that particular ice cream. You're still too young. How about one with strawberries and nuts?"

"Okay, but it's for my father. He won't be happy about this."

"Then send your father here. I can't give you what you ordered."

"But the rum in the ice cream is fake anyway!" Malte complained.

"Still." The seller handed him a strawberry-nut ice cream. Malte morosely accepted the ice cream and trotted back to the deck with a grim face. What a meanie. In a high arc, the ice cream flew into the Wadden Sea.

They finally arrived. Frank Maybach was pleasantly surprised by the hallig. For the past ten years, he had lived with his family in Husum, but Grienoog was new to him. In the distance, he caught sight of the white shining haubarg, and the buildings scattered in front of it. He pulled out his phone and pulled up the beeper app. After hitting a few buttons on his display, he called up the Report Arrival button and called the hotel.

Meanwhile, his son sat on the jetty and waved at the boat, which was heading towards Föhr, leaving behind a foaming wake.

"Malte, please be careful," he admonished him, adding, "You know your mother doesn't like it when your clothes are wet."

"Yes, Dad, I know Mom doesn't like it when my clothes get wet."

Frank winked at his wife. They sat on the bench at the pier and waited under a hot, almost cloudless sky. Marianne looks really good today, he thought. Tanned brown and svelte, with everything where it should be. Her short red hair showed the first strands of gray. As he lit a cigarette, she shot him a scathing look.

"Frank!" she exclaimed with a flash of her green eyes.

"Dad, smoking is unhealthy!" crowed his son from the jetty.

Maybach took one more drag from the cigarette and exhaled with a sigh. The car would have to be slow, he thought as he leaned back against the bench. Nearby, sheep were bleating. Standing at the fence and watching the people, they were whiling away their time chewing their cud instead of eating grass. Sheep have it good, Frank mused, thinking of the coming negotiations on the hallig. Eating and sleeping, and now and then a little bit of pooping. Well, slaughter was part of life too; after all, he also ate mutton from time to time.

He was planning to meet with a representative of a wind power company, a certain man named Wolters. So far, they had only been in touch on the phone. He had copies of all the relevant documents in one of the suitcases sitting on the jetty. He went through all the arguments once again in favor of the Savonius rotors. Actually, there were no cons in this case: no noise as was true with the conventional, horizontally mounted rotor blades, only a quiet whisper. And thanks to the innovative idea of an employee, they had achieved an increase in efficiency of eighty percent.

A small car now appeared, quietly whizzing along the narrow road with nothing more than just a whir and the crunch of the tires on the sandy ground. He called to his son and finally stood up.

A startlingly cheerful hotel employee jumped out of the runabout, on whose hood the ghost rider logo of the Hotel Deichvogt was emblazoned at a large scale.

"Moin, Moin! Welcome to Grienoog!" The man stretched his massive hand toward the Maybachs.

"Moin! Once is enough," called Malte.

"Sure, it is," grunted the friendly employee, who went on to introduce himself: "My name's Knut, like the polar bear from the books." The luggage was quickly stowed, and after a five-minute drive they pulled up at the hotel, an imposing building that towered into the summer sky. Malte was so amazed he couldn't speak; his parents were also impressed. Swallows flitted around the roof, and soft music floated like a dream from somewhere.

They were greeted just as warmly in the foyer as they had been at the jetty. After the usual hotel instructions, they went to their room. What a view! And the bathroom! Frank quickly figured out how to operate the state-of-the-art shower, as did his wife and Malte. The parents were surprised at how long their son could take in the shower. Their reminder that water is a precious resource and must be used carefully for the sake of the environment was the only thing that stopped the humorous dispute between the automatic system and their bright son.

That evening, they sat at dinner with a woman who had to be "ancient," as Malte whispered to his parents.

HOTEL
First day after the storm
3 p.m.

NEXT IN LINE FOR QUESTIONING WERE MRS. AND MR. Sieversten, two rather nondescript individuals, in Kollerup's opinion. Inconspicuous and both sand dune-type seniors. He wore a summer shirt that may have been fashionable in the eighties. She wore a dress in beige, just like a sand dune. As soon as Kollerup saw her, he imagined her in a sketch done by a well-known cabaret artist, who teasingly chided people who chose beige as the color of summer.

After the introductions, the recording of their identities, and the question about where they were at the time of the presumed crime, Kollerup's questions turned personal.

"Is this your first time to this hallig?"

"Yes. Terrible what happened in such a beautiful place!" Kurt Sieversten seemed shocked by the death of the mudflat guide; his wife was also visibly shaken. With a sad face, she said, "You wouldn't wish such a death on anyone, on such a night. And so—" she searched for a suitable word, "suddenly."

"Can you imagine someone causing what happened?"

Kollerup wanted to shake them both up a little, but all he got was widened eyes in response.

"Who would want—" Heidi Sieversten struggled to speak. "After all, we were all at dinner!" Her husband couldn't imagine such a thing either. One of the guests? Impossible.

"Where were the staff? Have you checked their alibis?" he asked the inspector.

"We aren't certain of that yet," Kollerup explained succinctly. "Do you have any children?" The question sounded quite nonchalant. The couple glanced at each other awkwardly. Mrs. Sieversten sighed and said, "Yes, we had a daughter. She died forty years ago in a car accident. The driver was never found."

At that moment, there was a knock on the door.

"Come in!" ordered Kolle.

The hotel manager.

"I need to talk to you," he said, and you could tell it was important. Kollerup apologized to the Sieverstens. "We're finished here. Or do you have anything else to add?" The two of them shook their heads.

Outside the door, Budnik whispered. "We have established a connection with the mainland. I wanted you to be the first to know about it."

"Nice!" Kolle praised him. "Let's go to your office." Once there, he dialed the number of the Husum police office. Busy. He repeated the process several times, until someone finally picked up. His colleague Larrson! After a short greeting, Kollerup filled him in on what had happened over the past two days.

His colleague was clearly happy to know that Kollerup was safe and sound. Then he reported: "We currently have several buildings damaged in North Frisia; only a few people have been injured though, no deaths. On the islands and the other halligs, things look similar to where you are, boss. The dikes have held, though several sheep have died. There are several missing persons, but I think they'll eventually show up unhurt, thanks to the early storm warning. The jetties have done well so far too."

"Pay attention," Kolle interrupted the torrent of speech. "I urgently need information about the people I just mentioned. Also, about the deceased."

"Sure."

"Good."

"Anything else?"

"No. Send those things to me as an email attachment, so I can print them out. And everything as soon as possible, of course. "

"Alright, boss!"

FERRY
Two weeks before the storm
2 p.m.

CHRISTA WAS LOOKING FORWARD TO A VACATION AND her new task. She sat relaxed on the sundeck of the Sandcrab and enjoyed the warm sun, the wind, and the vastness of the Wadden Sea. The hotel on the hallig seems interesting, she thought, as she skimmed through the information about the Deichvogt in the brochure. "The Deichvogt. The perfect symbiosis of high-tech and tradition awaits you." Well, she decided the promise sounded a bit exaggerated. The photos showed a normal though imposing haubarg sitting atop a mound. The brochure failed to explain what counted as extremely modern about the facility. The only commentary was this: "Apart from the usual things which one should expect from a top-class hotel, the Deichvogt represents the unusual." All the amenities were listed on two pages farther back in the booklet. Among the many things one would usually expect at this price point, an "interactive shower head with voice-activated temperature control" was mentioned. She thought this sounded funny and imagined having a conversation with a shower about water temperature and flow strength.

She grabbed her rolling suitcases as the loudspeaker told passengers to get ready to disembark. Waiting at the bow, she felt the envious glances of the other women at her back. Age had been kind to her so far. At the pier, she hailed the hotel's e-taxi, which arrived driven by a young man. Too many muscles, in her opinion, but otherwise quite nice. She was here on business, though. This wasn't a time to make male acquaintances; she had other things on her mind, specifically her orders.

Christa had decided to arrive two weeks before the actual reason for her stay. This gave her time to get an idea of the surroundings and the location. Besides, as the hotel owner had told her at the reception desk, she was their only guest for the first week of her visit. All the better. A little walking, relaxing and studying of the documents in peace. Her goal was set: she had to convince her contact person out of a product. She could do that. After all, as her ex-boss had once asserted, she was "the best horse in the stall." While working for a US wind turbine manufacturer in Hamburg, she had distinguished herself by her ability to guide difficult negotiations to success. She had, thus, risen to become the right hand of her ambitious boss. She'd had a brief fling with her boss's son, which had ended when his father arranged for him to marry the daughter of a financier in the States. By the late 1990s, she'd left her job and received a large severance package. With her family's inheritance and the company's money, she was set and didn't have to worry about making a living. After that, she'd worked as a freelance consultant for companies in the wind industry as a means to keep from being bored to death. She lived well and expensively. She never let the grass grow under her feet and was always looking for a new challenge. That was also the case now with this contract from a client who had promised her a handsome commission.

Contrary to her expectations, she actually enjoyed the outstanding hotel on the hallig. She passed the time with long walks and regular visits to the gym. How small the world is, she thought wistfully, as she once stood at the water's edge and looked toward the island of her birth: Föhr. The world was tiny, as she'd had to learn years ago as a teenager, and the mainland was far away. In her youth, she'd envied the others of her age who'd had the world at their feet. At least, that was how it had seemed to her as a girl.

Every young person had their problems with the North Frisian coast of the North Sea. In Hamburg, everything was different! Moving away from Föhr to study business administration on the Elbe river had been her liberation. After a year in the metropolis, Föhr was a foreign planet she never wanted to set foot on again. Her parents had sent her money regularly, so that she didn't have to work part-time. At Christmas, she'd visited her parents, but by early January, she was always happy to finally be able to trade her dreary family home for her life in Hamburg. In the summer months, she'd hitchhiked with her friends from her university to Spain or Greece, but she'd never let her goal out of her sight: one day she would be nicely settled in an extremely nice house with a husband and children. For that, she had to study hard and make a career as soon as possible. While her friends at the university had other things on their minds than their studies, she had been an ambitious student.

Then she'd met Kai Wolters; their paths had crossed during one of her Christmas visits to Föhr. They had known each other from their school days together, but had shown no interest in each other back then. However, on that December day when they'd met by chance, she'd suddenly found him very attractive. He was about to move to Hamburg to study electrical engineering and economics. He'd wanted to become a politician, and although he didn't know exactly what his path would be, he'd thought economics was a good start.

So, when Kai had arrived in Hamburg, they'd moved in together. That time had been wonderful, until one day they'd had a terrible fight. He had turned into a stranger to her, with his ambitious plans to become a politician. He had tried unsuccessfully to make a name for himself in several parties, but had ultimately ended up in an extreme left-wing party. The friction between them had increased when it came to fundamental issues. He was radical, while she had been a more mainstream liberal and had just wanted to live a comfortable life. Like his left-wing buddies, he'd wanted to see radical change in Germany, while she'd wanted it to stay the same. They'd argued about this, and one day she'd kicked Kai out of their shared apartment. After that, they'd lost track of each other.

All this flashed through her mind when she caught sight of Kai on her third day on the hallig. She almost didn't recognize him. A stocky figure with a slight paunch, and no trace of the person she had known all those years ago. All that remained of the old Kai was his grin and springy gait. His clothes had also changed with the times; you adapted to your age and peers.

Wolters seemed to recognize her immediately where she stood among a crowd of day visitors, ready to go on a guided mudflat hike. He continued his introduction after a brief hesitation, and they trudged off. After a few yards in the mud, he came up to her, a broad grin on his face.

"Christa?"

No, I'm the Easter Bunny, she thought. He then wrapped his still large arms around her. She didn't want to attract any undue attention and allowed him to squeeze her. With a noncommittal smile, she deliberately pushed him away when the moment was right.

"Yes, Kai. It's me. How are you doing these days? You're working as a mudflat guide now?"

"At our age, you have to supplement your pension somehow." He seemed to have noticed that she was more reserved than he had hoped. "You look good." However, he didn't look at her as he said this.

"You haven't changed a bit," she countered.

"You become realistic once you realize the world isn't going to change."

"No more revolutionary cells?"

That seemed to make him uncomfortable. His grin faltered, and a hard look stole into his eyes. They walked on without saying a word, accompanied by the muddy sound of their footsteps on the mudflats and the many-voiced babble of the group.

After a pause, he said only briefly, "No, things turned out differently."

That was all they had to say to each other. Kai returned to the group of visitors and resumed his tour of the mudflats. Eloquent and well-informed, he explained the special features of this environment and answered questions; after an hour, they reached a sandbank where they took a short break. The sun was blazing hot now, and one or the other of the guests rubbed sunscreen on their noses.

On the way back, Kai and Christa kept their distance from each other. When the group dispersed on their arrival at the hallig in the evening, Kai approached her.

"It would be nice if we could have a chat at the bar later."

Christa suddenly took pity on her old boyfriend and said, "In an hour?"

His smile reminded her of the time when she had fallen in love with him: "It's a date. See you then."

She spent the next hour reading. Lying on her bed in her room, she went through the documents of her mission. A delicate task this time. The target was married, and to make things harder, he would be coming with his wife. Those facts complicated things considerably. Kai Wolters was also a disruptive factor that had to be reckoned with and maybe even eliminated.

There was a yawning emptiness at the bar. The music in the background intensified this emptiness. Kai Wolters greeted her with, "What would you like to drink?"

She ordered a gin and tonic on the rocks, which perfectly matched the icy mood that now ensued.

"Well, what are you up to these days?" Apparently, he wanted to loosen up the tense atmosphere.

"I'm a freelancer now." She waited for him to reveal what

he wanted from her. "And you?" She looked straight at him. You've become fat, she thought. The slim lad had become a stocky retiree with a beer belly. And those clothes! Brown corduroy trousers, hiking boots, and a faded greenish gray summer shirt.

"You can see for yourself," he replied with a shrug, taking a sip of his drink to mask his embarrassment. "I've been a mudflat guide for ten years. It helps to round out my pension."

The only thing that interested her was why, after all these years, they just happened to run into each other on this hallig, back in their childhood region.

"You seem to be doing well," was the only thing she said, with a quick glance at his girth. He ordered another beer. Once it was sitting in front of him, he said, "It ended up going alright. My life, that is. After graduation, I had several jobs in the electrical industry. Munich and then Stuttgart. When my parents died about twenty years ago, I moved back up here." He studied his beer glass thoughtfully and rotated it in his hands. "I sold my parents' property—you know, the farm on Föhr. It brought good money. As an engineer at a wind turbine manufacturer, I had earned well, and—" he shrugged, "since I never got married and didn't have any children to pay for, I quit my job and went back to Föhr."

For a while, neither of them said anything. He then looked directly at her. "You haven't changed at all."

This made her strangely embarrassed, as she begrudgingly noticed. "Wind turbines, interesting," she said hastily to conceal her embarrassment. "Sounds like my own life." Her parents had left nothing behind, she reported. She'd had to work for everything. After graduation, she got a job in the States and stayed there. Married, but no children. Her husband had passed away fifteen years ago, leaving her his fortune. She kept to herself the fact that she now worked freelance for a company as a talent and innovation scout.

HOTEL
First day after the storm
3:30 p.m.

KOLLERUP WAS ABOUT TO HANG UP WHEN HIS colleague told him that Eysenhardt still wanted to talk to him. There was rustling on the line, then the prosecutor's usual commanding voice boomed out, "I was listening in, Kolle. Do what you want, and find the murderer. I'll take care of the rest. You have a free hand, at least until travel to the mainland is restored. You understand?"

Kollerup didn't really understand what he meant, but nevertheless he said in a jaunty tone, "Oui, mon General." Eysenhardt had, meanwhile, hung up. This race to be the first at the scene of a homicide was an old game between him and the prosecutor. This time the point went to the inspector.

His stomach started growling, so he went to look for Onne and found him in the bar with a plate on which a potato was desperately clinging to its rim. It had little chance against the superiority of the steak, which was pushing the meager vegetables to the side. "I'll have the same!" he called out as he swung onto the stool.

"They ran out a few minutes ago." Onne grinned, then waved off his comment. "Only joking."

Two women were sitting in the restaurant. Kollerup considered them. Oh, yes, Ms. Schneider and Ms. Koch. He then recalled that he still needed to go through the dead man's things. Arne, the cook, brought him his food and asked, "A beer to go with it, Inspector?"

Kollerup glanced at him and said dryly, "No, I still have to do a little detecting." The cook found this funny and laughed.

"Already have a lead, Inspector?"

"Nope. May I eat now?" Kolle didn't feel like talking about his work on an empty stomach. Besides, his head was still buzzing from last night. "Do you have something important to do?" he asked Onne between bites. As he ate, he was trying not to imagine how this huge portion had completely disappeared into the body of his friend, who measured only forty-seven inches tall. At this juncture, Onne pushed the last forkful into his mouth, chewed for a long moment, swallowed, and breathlessly exhaled, "Whew!" He stretched before continuing. "Why?" he asked idly as he picked his teeth with a toothpick.

"Because we need to go through the things from the dead man's pockets."

"We?"

"Yeah. I appoint you as my assistant. You've been very helpful, but now we can proceed officially."

"I can help you with that; the sheep can manage on their own now. And I can't continue with my art projects unless I switch completely to paint made from sheep dung." Onne considered this for a moment. "Not a bad idea... a little oil mixed with the manure... I could create color nuances through the feed..."

"ONNE! I am still eating!"

"You're too fat as it is, Kolle!" But then Kolle's new friend recalled what they had been talking about. "Sure. What should Watson do for you, Mr. Holmes?"

"Go get—" when he saw Onne cock one eyebrow, Kolle sat up straighter and continued, "...please go get the bags with the dead man's things."

"Very gladly, Kolle."

"Thank you."

In an unoccupied room, Kolle spread the items on a table, while Onne mounted the digital camera on a tripod.

"Well, let's see..." Kolle murmured, then more clearly, "A phone. A ballpoint pen. A notepad."

He leafed through it with hands clad in disposable gloves from the hotel kitchen. "Empty," he noted.

"Then... oh... a shrink-wrapped condom!"

"With banana flavoring!" Onne crowed.

Resignedly, Kolle raised his hands and whispered, "A little more professionalism, Onne. A little more."

"I'm now turning the phone on," Kolle pressed around the display until it came to life.

"A good device!" Onne exclaimed enthusiastically. It was still functional after all it had been through. Kolle silenced him with a murderous look.

"The last dialed numbers—" Kollerup murmured. "Aha! Three numbers." He read off the numbers for the camera, and just to be sure, he also wrote them down. He would check on these later.

"The deceased also has a bunch of keys in his pocket. Several small ones, two larger ones. And one ancient-looking key with a short piece, like the ones that were used before security locks were invented..."

"That's one of the keys for the old church!" Onne interrupted the accounting.

"The key for what old church?" Kolle was at a loss.

"That's the key I've been missing for a while."

"Alright. And?"

"It was around the time I found the two beer bottles in the mudflats. It must've slipped out of my pants' pocket at some point, and I gave up on ever finding it."

"But you had a second key?"

"Yeah, of course."

"But you don't recognize these other keys?"

"Let's see. This one..." Onne held one up, "could be the one for the staff quarters, where Wolters was allowed to stay in case of an emergency if he couldn't get off the island with his boat."

"Why would that have been?"

"It has happened before. During a storm, or when the water didn't recede fast enough. Does that make sense? Too high to walk to Föhr, or too low to go by boat."

"Alright. And the other keys?"

"I don't recognize them." Onne shook his head regretfully. Since the notepad had also yielded nothing, Kolle ended the examination. Time for a break, he decided.

"I'm going to stretch my legs. Could you go find Budnik and ask him if he knows what the other keys are for?"

"Sure." Onne grabbed the keys and disappeared.

Outside, the hotel employees were cleaning up the mess. The first thing they did was clear the paths using the electric scooters, which, equipped with trailers, provided valuable services. At the pier, which had been provisionally repaired by Jan-Ole and Maik, they heaped up large piles of garbage and separated the types of materials: plastic, compostable waste, and a third pile for stuff that didn't fit into the other categories. Activity was buzzing all across the hallig, but the sheep grazing on the meadow seemed to be unconcerned. Some were simply hanging around the fence and watching the strange things the people were up to.

Kolle sat down at the water's edge on a wooden chair that just happened to have been washed up there. He found it immensely practical and thanked the storm god, if there happened to be one. The Wadden Sea lay shrouded in mist in front of him. A light breeze was blowing in from the mainland, and a pale sun was fighting its way through the fog. The temperature had dropped significantly compared to last week, but the seabirds still weren't back yet. There was also nothing to be seen or heard from the sparrows, which usually fought with the seagulls over the tidbits in the sheep droppings. Only the swallows were flitting around once more at almost break-neck speed over the meadows.

He pulled out the dead man's phone that was still in the bag he had brought with him. Pulling up the list of calls, he dialed the first number. There was a crackling sound on the line, and then the ringing started. At the same moment, a familiar commercial ringtone started to go off somewhere near the hotel. Kolle stood up and listened—over there! Now I am curious, thought the inspector. Someone answered the call.

"Hello!" sounded from the speaker—a female voice. In a group at the pier stood a woman with a phone pressed to her ear. A dark-haired woman in a jumpsuit. I wouldn't push her out of bed, Kolle thought with a grin—wide hips and a considerable bustline. From a distance, she was quite pretty, with her slanting eyes and a mischievous smile on her face, which currently reflected both impatience and disapproval. A smaller blonde woman was speaking to her. He could only catch snatches of what she was saying into the phone. The tall one grunted, "Hey, you sicko! Is this your idea of fun?"

Kolle could hear the smirk in her voice as she held out the phone so that the other woman could listen in. Kollerup was enjoying the situation.

"Moin. This is Chief Inspector Kollerup, currently on the hallig, Grienoog. If you look to the left, you can see me."

Both women's jaws dropped when they caught sight of him. Recognizably taken by surprise, they waved in response.

"I'll be right over!" Kolle continued before hanging up.

The two women couldn't have been more different: one tall, strong and black-haired; the other petite and blonde. Both were as pretty as a picture, and Kolle wondered if they were models. Both were in jumpsuits bearing the logo of the hotel on the breast pockets. Kolle had to force himself not to look at the opened zipper of the dark-haired one as he awkwardly introduced himself.

"Moin. Kolle... eh, my name is Kollerup, Chief Inspector Kollerup."

Both women smiled at him, and his heart slipped to the back of his knees. They shook hands, and the tall one held his hand a fraction of a second too long for it to be a coincidence. The blonde was shy and only lightly brushed his fingers.

"Moin. Mine's Franziska Koch. This is—" the dark one gestured toward her fellow traveler, "Ilona Schneider, my partner."

Oops. Kolle's heart rumbled across the asphalt of the road towards the sea.

Ilona laughed and declared, "And she's my partner too!"

"Oh!" Kolle tightened his jaw. Are they pulling my leg? It wasn't unheard of for women to preemptively fake a lesbian relationship to protect themselves against unwanted advances. He thought he had read that somewhere.

"What can we do for you, Mr. Kollerup?" Franziska took charge. Fine, thought Kollerup. Now we know who's the dominant one in the relationship.

"Uh... how come the dead man had your number in his phone? Did you contact him before you arrived?"

The tan on Schneider's face paled slightly, while Franziska Koch pulled out a pack of cigarillos and nervously lit one.

"Are we suspects now?" At the end of her question, she blew the smoke out through her strawberry-pink, O-shaped lips. Delicate circles floated out into the still air. My goodness! Kollerup asked himself for the umpteenth time why people ever thought repeating dialogue from crime shows was a good thing. All you had to do was respond with the standard phrase, "At this time, everyone is a suspect." Of course, every interviewee's goal was to gain time this way; that was obvious. However, he now shamelessly exploited Koch's gambit by doing what was never expected of a real policeman: he forged ahead.

"At this stage of the investigation, I have to assume that everyone is a suspect. Pure routine. If you're innocent, you have nothing to fear."

Ms. Schneider giggled. Her partner squinted one eye shut, as if calculating her odds of coming out on top in this battle of the stereotypes.

"I called him, yes. Must've been last week."

"For private or business reasons?"

"Private."

"What did you want from him?"

"That was private, so none of your business."

"We have a dead man on our hands. Everything's my business now."

"I've forgotten."

"But you remember it was private?"

"I only make private calls from my cell phone."

"And if you get a business call?"

"Dear Inspector, then it would be business, don't you think?"

"What business did you have to discuss with the dead man?"

"Who says he called me?"

"His list of dialed numbers."

"Who says I talked to him... oh... the call duration."

"You learn fast, madame."

Her partner now came to the rescue. "Mr. Wolters refused to take a hint! He constantly calls... called, and all Franziska wanted to do..."

Franziska interrupted her. "Stop talking, Ilona!"

Although Kollerup had his own thoughts on the matter and considered their conversation still incomplete, he said, "I would like to ask you both to make yourselves available at the hotel in half an hour." Then he strolled back to the Deichvogt without bidding them goodbye. After a few steps, he heard a heated argument break out between the two. Ilona was apparently being bawled out by her girlfriend.

FERRY
Three days before the storm
11:30 a.m.

FRANZISKA SAT IN THE SUN, LETTING HER SKIN SIZZLE
on the sun deck of the transport boat to the hallig. She wore
only a bikini top and snug short jeans pants. Her already deep
brown skin, spanning her voluptuous body, corresponded
delightfully, she thought, with her partner Ilona's blonde hair.
The latter lay with her head in her girlfriend's lap, popping
her bubblegum. She wasn't the type to get a tan and was
more likely to get sunburned. That was why her petite body
was completely clad in a one-piece summer jumpsuit that
revealed more than it hid.

Franziska now saw the hallig appear on the horizon in their
direction of travel. Gently running her fingers through her
partner's golden hair, she murmured lazily, "Ilona dear? We're
almost there. Could you take care of the luggage?"

As she bound her hair up into a braid, which got the attention
of the men on the ship, Ilona strolled down the stairs to the
lower deck, which drew just as many male stares. Franziska
slipped on a tight sweatshirt and lit a cigarette. The way it
looked at the moment, only a dead Wolters could have given
her what she had been working toward for years. Fortunately,
she had managed to win Ilona over, who had been able to
provide her with information directly from the source. The

employees of the tourist center in Husum were always on the cutting edge of the mudflat guide business.

The life of a tidal flat guide was hard. However, if you had the appropriate routes, it was an enjoyable part-time job. Moreover, she was used to getting what she wanted. And it was a cool side job, in her opinion. She loved the nature of the Wadden Sea, loved to show tourists how beautiful her home was. But just going out a hundred meters with whining children from the Husum dock, digging a hole, and coming back with a bucket of lugworms wasn't exactly her life's goal. She hadn't taken the long road to becoming a certified mudflat guide for that. The conquest of the delightful Ilona had been a gift from heaven. As head of the tourism center, she was like winning the lottery. She hadn't needed to woo her for too long; after only two weeks, they were in bed together. She had only revealed her plan to her partner bit by bit. Later, when Franziska was sure that Ilona was in love with her, she'd revealed her plans for their future. That had been in the fall of last year. Now they lived together and acted like a married couple.

As soon as she'd learned from Ilona that Kai Wolters was organizing a tour for the hotel guests from Grienoog, the decision had been quickly made: to the hallig or bust.

Panting, Ilona climbed up the steps, heavily laden, and set both backpacks down with a crash in front of Franziska.

"Whoa! What all did you bring along?" She had strapped her trekking backpack to her back and carried her partner's against her chest.

"Oh, only the basic essentials," replied Franziska. "A pair of dumbbells with interchangeable weights, my photo equipment and some nutritional supplements. And underwear, shoes and such..." she added, smiling. "After all, I want this to feel like a vacation." She tapped her shoulder bag. "And our plan on the tablet." Effortlessly, she lifted her backpack and squeezed her arms through the straps.

Then they were standing at the exit of the ferry and watching their destination approaching: the mound on which the massive haubarg stood.

As a precaution, Franziska ordered the hotel's electric vehicle before they docked so they would be in their rooms quickly. She wanted to swim in the North Sea before dinner.

The driver's flirtatious greeting bounced off them as if against a steel wall. Within seconds, the fellow knew he wouldn't score with either of them. Ilona and Franziska played the parts of entitled and excited vacationers, chattering away about the gorgeous panorama and giggling while pointing out the stupid sheep to each other.

They jumped out of the car like schoolgirls and dashed up the stairs to the reception, while a grumpy Knut cursed and struggled with the insanely heavy backpacks.

Their rooms were next to each other, the windows offering a breathtaking view! The seemingly endless Wadden Sea lay before them. A deep blue, cloudless sky arched above everything.

Someday I'll be out there, leading people around and living an exciting life, Franziska vowed. The money will just flow. Once... yes, once all the hurdles have been cleared, then... She sighed and wrapped her arms around Ilona, who was blissfully gazing at the seeming paradise. "Didn't you want to go swimming?"

"Oh, yes." Already Ilona was scurrying through the connecting door into her room, literally discarding her clothes as she went. Franziska watched her with a grin.

While Ilona was turning the heads of the day guests, Franziska began to work out their joint plan. Having already found out that Wolters had a penchant for young blonde women, her partner was supposed to raise the hopes of the man during the mudflat hike. Ilona assumed that it wouldn't take much to make him bite. Then the first part of the plan could be carried out in the old church. There she would show up and seemingly take them unawares, and then demand to have three-way sex. If Wolters hesistated, she would threaten to make a big fuss about it and sell the story to the press as sexual assault.

At the appropriate moment, she would knock him out with a syringe full of anesthetic, which would allow them to deposit his defenseless body in the mudflats as the tide drained away. She knew her way around the area and was acquainted with where the tideways with strong currents were to be found. The ebbing current would do the rest. Problem solved.

After an excellent meal and a prolonged cuddle with Ilona, Franziska wanted to take a closer look at the church. The information on the internet was scanty, only mentioning that the building was now used as a sheepfold. She wanted to check things out in more detail. Thank God there were hardly any mosquitos here, Ilona told her with relief.

So they strolled leisurely along the paved paths of the hallig, past the miniature golf course, which was more like a full-sized golf course with eighteen generously-spaced holes. A hotel employee was passing the time there by trying to sink some putts. They stood at the fence and watched him sweat. With each successful stroke, they applauded dutifully and acknowledged each mistake with a prolonged cry of regret.

When he had abandoned his efforts, a couple arrived with a child, obviously wanting to show their bored son how fascinating the game could be, and the women moved on.

On a mound stood a building reminiscent of a castle made of gray stone. That it had once been a church could be seen from the generously proportioned entrance and the leaded windows, some of which showed biblical motifs. In contrast, at the entrance there was an unsightly extension made of cement pavers, which was probably intended to serve as a temporary rain shelter for the sheep. The gateway to the church must have collapsed many years previously. From the path they had an unobstructed view into the interior. Dusty streams of light fell on empty stalls and carelessly-thrown straw and hay bales. Next to the chapel, sheep grazed in a meadow. A cottage on an adjacent mound seemed to be inhabited by the shepherd; a rather puny-looking man in an undershirt and shorts was standing next to the wooden hut in front of an easel, obviously engrossed in his work.

He didn't notice that the two stunning women were interested in the architectural refinements of the former church. Likewise, it seemed to escape his notice that one of the ladies was snapping photos with her phone. Access to the church was barred by a typical sheep gate, which closed by itself as soon as you let go of it. On the crooked gate hung a sign warning of sheep droppings lying around. Access was not strictly forbidden, though hardly anyone would have dared to enter such a treacherously mined area.

When the women opened it, it squeaked pathetically, and the man turned around. Waving cheerfully, they greeted him, and the small man waved back with his paintbrush.

"Only the good parlor is open to visitors, but please wipe your feet first!" He chuckled at his joke and turned back to his painting. What a strange little man, Franziska thought in confusion. He seemed immune to the concentration of sex appeal that was gracing his stable.

Tiptoeing around the animal-laid mines, they stumbled inside, giggling. As usual, buildings like this appeared larger on the inside than on the outside. Apart from the pervasive, penetrating smell of the sheep, it was surprisingly tidy. Franziska could imagine that the nights could be passed in relative comfort on the hay bales. Swallows nested in the beams, constantly flitting about and feeding their brood. Franziska and Ilona strolled around the pleasantly cool stable and photographed the fading evidence of the former place of worship. Here a weathered figure, there an almost unrecognizable mural. One way or another, there was something saddening about seeing a house formerly used by Sunday visitors degenerating into a sheepfold. On the other hand, as Ilona remarked innocently, it was nice to see the same animals that had been present at the Savior's birth find a home. My goodness, Franziska thought, she really just said Savior! Sometimes her partner's naiveté got on her nerves. With a wink, she asked Ilona to give one of the hay bales a test run.

Just as her partner had started to make herself seductively comfy on the bale, a voice boomed from the entrance. Since the sun was beaming in at an angle, the startled women could only make out a dark shadow.

"I hope you're not messing things up in here. My sheep like their order!"

"IT'S NICE THAT YOU'VE COMPLIED WITH MY REQUEST," Kollerup began the conversation. A pair of sharp opposites, he thought, as he admired them both, now that they were both out of their shapeless overalls. Franziska Koch was obviously the dominant partner, while Ilona Schneider was the blonde, more naive one. While Koch appeared tall and athletic, Ilona was more delicate and girlish. Both were stunningly attractive and exuded extreme sexual charisma. If Kollerup hadn't already known he wouldn't stand a chance with either of them, he would have been the first to shoot any other admirer just to hop into bed with one of them.

"You knew the dead man?"

His gaze wandered back and forth between the two.

Ilona reacted first. "Just because we called the mudflat guide? Are we suspects now, or what?"

"Ah," Franziska Koch smiled mildly, patting one of her partner's delightful knees. "My dear Chief Inspector Kollerup, we just had a question for Mr. Wolters."

Kollerup nodded knowingly and said, "Must have been a tricky question. Your conversation lasted five minutes."

"It was a complicated question that he couldn't answer just like that."

"Go into a little more detail."

"I wanted to know if we could take something from the mudflats, like relicts from sunken settlements or stuff like that."

"And you can't just put them in your pocket. You have to be an official archaeologist to do that!" Ilona nodded vigorously to her comment.

"I see. How stupid of me," Kollerup muttered.

"Yes... well..." Franziska nodded her head thoughtfully. "I then handed the phone off to my partner, because he needed some personal information from her."

"What did he want to know?" Kolle looked at Ilona.

"Oh... he wanted to go out with me, but I turned him down." At this, she glanced at Franziska with a wink.

Kollerup nodded and considered his next question. "What do you two do for a living?"

Franziska answered, "I work at Kohn's, as a sales clerk."

Kollerup nodded at Ilona in an inviting manner.

"Me? Uh... yes... at the Husum tourist office."

"Have I already asked where you both were at the presumed time of Wolter's death?"

"Is this an official interrogation or a casual questioning?" Franziska was now visibly nervous.

"Nothing official, just routine." Kolle smiled reassuringly, raising his hands apologetically, and adding innocently, "This is only for my report. The prosecutor is very demanding; everything has to be just so." Kollerup was pleased he'd thought to say this.

"I know that phrase," Ilona exclaimed excitedly. "The inspector in that series... Columbus or something... always says that."

"Ilona," her partner looked at her pityingly. "This isn't a TV series." At that, she shook her head and sighed. "Was that everything? Mr..." she raised an eyebrow mockingly and continued in a clearly ironic tone, "...Inspector? Or do you have one last question?"

"No, that's it for now."

When the two were about to leave the room, he called after them. "Where were you when Wolters collapsed in front of the veranda window?"

The couple turned around. They both looked momentarily guilty, then got themselves under control again.

"In the dining room. We had just placed our orders on the tablet. Come on, Ilona," Franziska started to pull her partner out.

"Just a minute!"

Kolle just wanted to impress upon them the need to keep themselves available for further questioning, but realized how stupid that would sound.

"Leave the door open." He couldn't think of anything better to say.

He glanced at his watch. Coffee break.

Onne was sitting in the restaurant, devouring a huge piece of cake. "You want a piece too?" he mumbled with his mouth full.

"No, thanks. Only coffee."

Onne pointed vaguely with his thumb and watched Kolle questioningly.

"There's something..." Kollerup thoughtfully strolled to the bar and ordered a coffee. "Black without sugar, and..." he added with his finger raised, "... freshly brewed."

"But that's going to take a while," grumbled the cook, fiddling with the equipment in protest.

"I'm in no hurry," Kollerup muttered.

"There's something that I don't understand," the inspector completed his sentence as he sat down next to Onne.

"There are several things I don't understand," Onne sighed.

Kolle summarized what they had so far, which actually wasn't all that much. But, he reassured himself, they were at the very beginning of their investigation, and who knew what would come out in the end.

Maybach and his family were still on the list for questioning, and he also needed to ask the retired couple more questions. Wolters had apparently not endeared himself to the people who had been in close contact with him. The stylish retired administrative assistant was holding something back, and the pair of women seemed to be hiding a lot.

"Let's see what comes out of the Maybachs," he concluded his thoughts.

Onne now pulled out the dead man's keychain.

"Budnik and his wife were able to identify two of these. One is, as I already suspected, from the employees' lodge. The other big key is actually to the church door. This one..." he held one up that looked like a key for a bicycle lock, flat with a long, angled bit, "...is for his bicycle. An ancient Dutch bicycle. Sits in a shed behind the hotel."

Now Onne triumphantly held up the last one.

"Now this one is the interesting one. Too small for a door key, too big for a cash box or something, don't you think?"

"I see," Kolle knew immediately what Onne was getting at. "That means Wolters didn't have a key for his own house on Föhr."

Onne grumbled, "You ruined my punch line."

"Sorry. But there is something else that's strange."

"Tell me, Mr. Holmes!" Kolle's friend looked at him with wide eyes. Kolle counted with his fingers: "Keychain, phone, and a blank notebook."

"Yes, and?" Onne seemed at a loss.

"Shall I show you what I have in my pockets?" As he said this, the Inspector was already spreading their contents on the table. Onne was speechless.

"MacGyver would be proud of you."

"You never know what might happen." For Kolle, it was completely normal to carry his ID card along with his Swiss army knife, a lighter and cigarettes. Then, of course, he carried tissues, a bag of licorice, a chocolate candy, a yellowed receipt (one year old), and a slip of paper with passwords and credit card PINs. "The rest is in the room safe," he finished his review. He looked at Onne knowingly.

"So, he must have deposited something in the staff lodge before his death."

"Sounds logical."

They decided that Onne should go to Wolter's room and see what the safe could reveal, while Kolle would question the Maybach family and look for the Sieverstens again. They agreed they would compare notes in the evening, which would give Onne time to take care of some personal tasks. Before they parted the Inspector remembered: "What's up with those strange bottles of yours?"

"They're over in the lodge, in the safe."

"Yes, great. But where did the bottles come from?"

"I got them... well..." Onne shook his head, "twenty years ago now, found them in the old church. That was when the stone altar was still there. It was in my way, and underneath I found a cavity where these two bottles were sitting."

"The pastor's secret reserve?"

"I don't know. The last pastor left Grienoog in 1960. By the nineties, it was used as a sheepfold."

"How old do you estimate the bottles to be? And..." Kolle raised a finger, "can we still drink what's in them?"

"No way! They're at least a hundred years old. I researched this at the time. Undrinkable."

"A hundred years!" Kolle marveled.

"Yes, maybe. It's also possible that there was once a small brewery here that sank during a storm tide. Or the good Theo Storm lost them here during his hallig trip," the painterly shepherd added with a grin.

"Let's talk about this some more tonight." Kollerup stood up, and Onne followed him.

Surprisingly, as far as Kolle could see, order had been returned to the hallig. From the mound, they could see electric cars flitting back and forth between the jetty and the work sites with full and empty trailers. Obviously, in addition to the employees, the guests were also helping out. His tongue hanging out, the Maybachs' son was aimlessly dragging a stone around, which every adult had to admire. The hotel manager was walking around with a notebook and giving instructions.

Onne strode toward the staff lodge while Kolle headed toward Budnik with his hands buried in his pockets. Kollerup decided to renounce his ability to play the bumbling detective, an act he had perfected over the years. He was on duty!

"Moin, Mr. Budnik! It looks really good already!"

"Ah, Inspector, moin! I'm doing my best to organize everything." Budnik wiped a non-existent film of sweat from his forehead. "It's good that you're here." He reached into the car behind him and handed Kolle several thick stacks of papers wrapped in transparent pouches. "They arrived when you were questioning the guests."

Kolle was astonished. His colleagues, above all his assistant Larsson, had put in a lot of effort. He stood there indecisively with the packets, before deciding there was still time and asking the manager where he could find the Maybachs. Budnik reached back into the vehicle and consulted a list. Kollerup tried to squint at the sheet, but all he saw were illegible scribbles, crosses and checks.

"Back there. By the mini golf course." The hotel manager jabbed his pen in the direction the inspector should go. The inspector gratefully declined the manager's offer to drive him there.

The Maybachs were busy working with Nele to make the course playable again. Malte wandered up with his stone, which he had in the meantime presented to each of those present for inspection, and handed it to his mother, who, without comment, tossed it over the fence. When her son started to protest, Kollerup stepped through the opening in the fence, and all eyes were on him.

"Moin, Nele! I have to kidnap your helpers. They won't be gone long."

The Deichvogt overalls looked delightful on her. She had cinched in the waist, which emphasized her feminine figure. "It isn't as bad here as outside the fence." She waved. She was right about this, because stuck to the fence were all kinds of plastic debris, seaweed, algae, and branches of brushwood.

At the golf course, there was a tool shed with an office, which was surprisingly undamaged. Only one window had been destroyed by a branch.

Kollerup pointed to the building. "I think we can sit down in the little building over there."

MINIATURE GOLF COURSE
First day after the storm
5 p.m.

THE TOOL SHED WAS ADEQUATE FOR THE PURPOSE. Two tables with chairs, and on the walls, aerial photos of the Wadden Sea. In one corner, boxes with drinks. On a shelf, neatly lined up, several drinking glasses. Next to the door, a desk, and a window with a view of the golf course.

The Maybachs entered with their son and took their seats.

"I don't think we need your son just yet," Kollerup said, and the boy's mother sent him out to Nele.

Kolle had thought to put the tablet he had been using for his investigation into a shoulder bag, and after both the Maybachs didn't object, he began recording their interview.

"We were sitting in the dining room when Wolters collapsed at the window."

Frank Maybach, a slim yuppie type, spoke with a slight Swabian accent. Though he tried to speak clearly and without accent, he couldn't hide his homeland. Marianne Maybach, a typically athletic, motherly housewife, was wearing a dignified outfit. She looked like the type who wore quilted, shiny vests in pink or gold in the fall. Her husband was wearing a trenchcoat, with a matching wide-brimmed hat of the same material.

Boring people like this usually had little to do with a murder, as Kollerup knew. Nevertheless, he asked them what connected them both to Wolters. Such people were usually proper in their behavior, but they were also easy to see through when caught in a lie. Frank Maybach spoke first, "Oh, yes... we know him from a mudflat hike. Isn't that right, Marianne?" Marianne nodded, staring out the window.

"Ah, yes. Do you know a Mrs. Hansen? Christa Hansen? She's one of your fellow guests."

Whoosh! A chameleon would be proud of the frenzied color change that the couple now showed. White, red, suntan alternated in fractions of a second.

"Well, Inspector," Mark Maybach hemmed and hawed. "Wolters... I actually wanted to meet with him."

"Why?"

Kolle didn't like it when people used actually like this. It was often deployed as an excuse to be imprecise, to keep quiet about something, or drag out an explanation in order to make the speaker seem important. In his opinion it ranked right below the sentence, "Guess what I found!"

"Well, yes," Maybach continued, "I'm an engineer, and I had planned to discuss a business proposition with the dead man... when he was still alive, that is. But it didn't happen because the mudflat tour was cancelled."

"Could you also tell me what you wanted to discuss?"

"Wolters worked for a company in the wind power industry as a so-called liaison. He advertised it on his official website."

"What does an liaison do?"

"He establishes contacts between developers and companies."

"Doesn't every company have its own development department?"

"Not all of them. The established ones can afford it. Other less well-known and less efficient companies in the industry cannot. They look for innovative ideas through middlemen."

"Industrial espionage with a legal coating."

"You could call it that, but I would rather call it a technology transfer. Not every company opts for innovation that originated as an idea in its own department. If that were the case, these companies would expose themselves to the risk of chasing a flop. We engineers know this and try not to tilt at windmills."

"I see. You work out ideas that grow the bottom line."

"Exactly. That's why our industry is the way you know it today. Conventional, stuffy, experimentation-adverse. The experiments are left to the small companies."

"And you wanted to sell him something."

"Yes." Maybach was thawing the more he spoke on the subject. "I wanted to present him with a new generation of vertical turbine systems. A groundbreaking idea. Because I have namely..."

"I know," the inspector interrupted him. Kolle remembered the discussion with Ms. Hansen.

"Do you know Ms. Hansen?"

"Yes. She had called me. That's why I also wanted to meet with her. You should always keep your options open in our business."

"Did Ms. Hansen know that you wanted to meet with Wolters?"

"If she did, she didn't learn it from me."

Kolle thought for a moment. Maybach wanted to see who would pay the most for his new development. Wolters and Hansen knew each other, but apparently didn't know of their mutual acquaintances. Hansen, an official representative of a US company and hopeful for a fat commission, and Wolters, a free agent who worked for anyone who would pay enough. And between them Maybach, who also hoped for a good deal and only had to wait to see who would make the highest bid. Greed, plain and simple. But Wolters was out of the running, which meant that now Hansen's company would have a good chance.

"Were there any other interested parties?"

"Not so far. I had wanted to give local companies from northern Germany a chance first."

"But didn't you know that Ms. Hansen works for a US company?"

This seemed to be the first time Maybach had heard this information.

"No!"

Kolle could tell this was an honest response. Well, he might have just derailed a new technical development, he thought regretfully.

"But that isn't a problem." The engineer waved it off. "There are other companies that would be interested. Wolters isn't, uh, wasn't the only broker in northern Germany. I'll just have to search the internet, and find someone else open to new ideas."

"Where were you when Wolters collapsed?"

"In the dining room. With my wife and Malte."

"And before that?"

"On the beach with my family."

Marianne Maybach, who had been listening the whole time, confirmed it. The inspector pushed his chair back and said abruptly, "That's it... for today." With that, he stood up and said goodbye.

It was time for him to consider all he had learned and finally read the printouts that his colleague Larsson had sent from Husum.

He left the mini golf course and searched for a quiet corner on the hallig where he could think undisturbed. This wasn't all that easy, since people were cleaning up everywhere. The electric cars were zooming all around, but despite the general busyness, it still looked like a demo effort pursued by bored hooligans.

There was a golden light over everything, created by the haze the sun had to fight its way through. In the complete silence, scattered sheep bleated, adding to the sense of being cut off from the rest of the world.

A vehicle whizzed up silently and stopped right next to him. Onne sat at the wheel with his arm casually hanging out.

"Hey! Taxi!"

"Yes. To the church, please."

"It's not on my route, but what the heck... I'm on a break anyway."

Kolle got in and clutched his seat as the car took off before he could buckle up.

"Hold on!" Onne shouted, accelerating as if he had to overcome the force of gravity in order to launch them into space toward Mars.

CHURCH
First day after the storm
5:30 p.m.

THREE SECONDS LATER, THE BREAK THRUSTERS FIRED, AND he nearly broke both arms when he crashed against the dashboard.

"Church!" Onne cheered and jumped out of the vehicle.

"Thank God, it's not the cemetery!" muttered Kollerup as he dropped to what he imagined was the red Martian surface.

"Funny," said Onne, squinting into a pale sun that was now struggling through the haze.

Kolle rolled to his knees and noticed that the sand truly was red. What the hell, he thought, and at the same moment he noticed the smell of iron. "Blood!"

Rusty brown sand stuck to his hands and knees, leaving annoying stains. Onne walked up, bent down, and sniffed knowingly.

"I guess, my dear Holmes, that we have the crime scene," he said in a nasal voice.

Kollerup now stood up and looked at the area. Some blood must have soaked the ground here, he thought before grabbing the tablet to take a photograph of it.

"Lie down next to it," he asked his friend.

"Are you...?" he protested, shaking his head in disbelief.

"Only to make a size comparison!" Kolle gestured at the ground impatiently.

"Nope. We'll do this another way." Onne pulled a folding ruler from the trunk of the car, unfolded it, and placed it next to the red stain. "Approximately one hundred eighty inches long and thirty-five inches wide."

Kolle carefully scratched around in the sand with his foot. After an inch and a half, the soil took on its normal color. He took one last photograph. Finally, he took a soil sample, which he stuffed into the cellophane wrapper from his cigarette pack.

"Mission accomplished," he said. Onne looked at him questioningly. Kolle waved him off and strolled around with his I know there's something hidden here look. The entrance to the church with its temporary porch made of cement pavers was three steps away. The roof, a piece of corrugated iron, lay on the meadow. Hadn't he examined it already? He had. He had found a piece of it earlier on his morning walk with Onne. No blood on it. Washed off by the rain. There was, except for the one spot here, no trace of blood anywhere. He considered this. What happens when an artery is cut at the neck? It spurts quite violently. How had Wolters been able to drag himself to the hotel in that weather? How had he escaped his killer, if it wasn't suicide?

What had happened? Wolters had been loitering here after nightfall in the approaching storm. Not unusual for a North Frisian, who must have experienced frightening weather before. What had happened on the night of his death, when Wolters must have been here, and how had a piece of corrugated iron gotten into the neck of the dead man?

Kolle was shaken on the arm by an alien.

"Earth to Mars! Anyone at home?"

"Say, you were out on the night of the murder," the inspector exclaimed. His friend looked at him perplexed before blinking twice. "Yes."

"Did you get to the hotel alone?"

"How..."

"Did someone get to the hotel just before you or after you?"

"No. After I locked the sheep in the chapel, I first went to my house, then straight to the hotel. It's brightly lit at night. It could pass as a light tower, because the façade is so well illuminated by floodlights."

"You didn't run into Wolters?"

"Nope. No one."

They were now in the church, which smelled like a sheepfold. There was no way to avoid the sheep droppings. Nevertheless, Kolle tried to tiptoe through with relative care. In the process, he kept a lookout for tracks. Annoyingly, the storm and rain had removed all traces. The sheep that had been let outside today had trampled everything flat. Only the blood-soaked path in front of the church testified to the fact that something had happened here, something that was related to the death of the mudflat guide.

A white scrap of paper caught his eye. It was lying on one of the bales of straw piled up against the church wall. Onne knew immediately what Kolle would ask for and held out a paper bag to him.

"Don't worry, they're new," he preempted Kolle's objection. "These are vomit bags from the boat."

The inspector sat down on a bale and pulled out the crumpled printouts he had been carrying around for a while.

"You could help me go through the documents." At this, he handed half of the printouts to his current assistant.

Larsson had done a good and fast job. How he missed him here, that slick-faced lout. With a surreptitious sideways glance at Onne, he silently apologized to his new friend who was the exact opposite of his usual assistant. But unusual times called for unusual measures, and artists certainly tended to have a good eye for detail.

Kolle began to skim through the printouts. He happened to be holding those of the guests while Onne had those of the employees.

When Kolle reached the Sievertsens' documents, he found something interesting. They had had a daughter who had died in a traffic accident in November 1983. The then thirteen-year-old had been hit by a vehicle at an intersection in Mildstedt and had died instantly. Some people out for a stroll had discovered the deceased child the following day. The perpetrator was never found, despite the greatest effort and assistance of the population.

Kurt Sievertsen had even offered a generous reward, but this only ensured that numerous people stepped forward to make accusations against their "strange neighbors" or others they didn't like.

The rest sounded like the resume of a successful businessman. Kurt's father had started a successful bakery, and his son had inherited it and built a small baking empire, which was known throughout North Friesland today.

Mrs. Sierversten's maiden name had been... wait a sec! Wolters! And she came from Amrum.

Hastily, Kolle pulled the dossier on the dead man and searched for his place of birth. Ha! Not Amrum, but Wyk on Föhr. As Kolle recalled, the hotel manager had said that Wolters had lived on Amrum and also on Föhr. It was a pity that the telephone lines were currently down, but he would try anyway. So, he pulled out his cell phone and... oh... the old flip phone. His tablet was in the refrigerator compartment of the minibar in his room. He had once heard that this would save the battery, and ever since then, he'd kept his phone and tablet in the fridge.

He would have to wait until he was back at the hotel to do some research online, assuming that the network was up again. He sighed. Everything used to be easier. You had kept all the important phone numbers in one book, without any need for batteries and search functions.

Now that he had the records on the dead man in hand, he looked to see what else was of interest.

All in all, what he read coincided with what he already

knew. Wolters had graduated as an electrical engineer, but had totally failed in economics. After that, he had worked as a development manager for an up-and-coming company that had focused on wind power. His parents, who at the time ran a well-established boarding house in Wyk, had died in the fall of 1983. He'd sold all their property, except for one house in which he spent intermittent holidays.

Now Kolle came across something worth noting. Wolters' aunt on his mother's side had married the brother of Heidi Sieversten's father. So, Mrs. Sieversten was related to the dead man's mother. Unbelievable! And she had really believed she could hide that?

CHURCH
First day after the storm
6 p.m.

"I'M GOING FOR A SMOKE," KOLLE MUTTERED.

"I'll come with you," Onne slid down from the straw bale and pulled out a flask.

"Want one too?"

"On duty?"

"You're on vacation, right?"

"Right."

"Hey!"

Onne had to snatch the flask back from him before it was empty.

"Tell me, Onne, what do you think about this?"

"It's like a real detective story!"

"Come on! Of course, it's a real detective story. A man is dead."

"Well, when you say it like that... I find it creepy. All the guests were in the restaurant. The only person hanging around outside was Wolters. But were all the guests and the employees really inside?"

"At the time of death, yes, except for the hotel technician. He was out dealing with the power outage. Shortly after the outage, we had power back, thanks to the generator."

"But I was also outside, Kolle. And I have no alibi."

"What motive would you have had?"

"Let's see... I'm a psychopath?"

"Oh, Onne."

"Well maybe the dead man wanted to get his hands on my valuable old beer bottles. After I had the sheep," he pointed to the old church, "in the barn, I went to my place, surprised Wolters as he rummaged around in the dark, and bang!"

"Yes, with a piece of corrugated iron!" Kolle snorted dismissively and rolled his eyes.

"Should I have stabbed him with a paintbrush?" Onne shrugged questioningly at that and continued. "Or scared him to death with a painting from the Brown Series?"

"I don't want to step on your toes, but Onne, you don't have the right temperament for a murder like this."

Onne pretended to be offended and folded his arms.

"Will your dossier reveal any connections to the dead man?" Kollerup asked between drags on his cigarette.

Onne seemed insulted. "Pshh!"

"Good grief! All right. I'm taking you into custody for the time being on the suspicion of Wolter's murder. Satisfied?"

"Just custody?"

"Just custody," confirmed Kolle seriously.

"And I am not too small?"

"No, Onne, you're not too small."

"No!"

"No, what?"

"There are no connections, except that Wolters has been the go-to mudflat guide here since the hotel opened, and he offered tours to the hallig visitors. So he automatically had contact with the employees, but also with the Budniks."

Kolle pondered. Sure, every employee had a connection to Wolters. He wondered whether all the "W-questions" could be answered. Who, what, when, where and why? What motive could the perpetrator have had, and who'd had the opportunity? They could leave out the "how "for a moment. Bled to death from a carotid artery injury. Whether poison or something else was involved could only be definitively determined once the results of the autopsy and the toxicological report were available.

Kolle explained what he had discovered. "If Mrs. Sieversten and Wolters were related, I should question the couple again." He then moved on to his interview with the Maybachs and his findings about the lesbian couple.

"I'd heard that Wolters fancied himself God's gift to women."

"Yes, Onne, but why? I mean..." he raised his arms helplessly, "he wasn't exactly an Adonis! Overweight, hot-tempered and over sixty." Kolle shook his head in despair.

"Kolle, let me tell you something: don't try to understand women. Many before you have failed at that. Or gone crazy trying." He circled his index finger meaningfully.

"Let's keep reading the documents." Kollerup glanced at his watch. "It'll be time for supper soon." In the meantime, the visibility had improved, and a light wind had picked up. The previously-pale sun continued to fight its way through, its warmth beginning to evaporate the moisture that lay across the hallig. The silence, which had been oppressive, was now interrupted by the tentative nibble of small waves. Up on the church mound, they could see all the way to the jetty. A sparrow fluttered through the grass and pecked at the grass seeds, and farther back on the meadow, a sheep bleated.

As they entered the church, Kolle's folding phone started to ring. Surprised, he accepted the call. He must be getting old. Hadn't he left it in his room? His colleague Larsson greeted him with his typical cool voice.

"Boss? Lührssen and Eysenhardt are on their way to meet you."

"What?"

"By helicopter."

Then the connection was interrupted. What the hell...?!

"What's happening?" Onne wanted to know.

"They'll be here shortly. Helicopter."

"Aliens?"

"Worse."

"Worse?"

"Coroner Lührssen and prosecutor Eysenhardt." A soft flapping sound could now be heard. "On the big H!" called Kolle.

"Big H?" asked Onne.

"Helicopter landing pad! Haven't you ever seen the big H on the ground?"

By now, all the hotel staff and guests had gathered at the landing site, nervously looking up at the pale blue sky. And there it came—the iron whirlybird. Goosebumps always ran down Kollerup's spine when a Bundeswehr helicopter landed. It reminded him of the images from his childhood and youth when the war in Vietnam had been reported on television. A song title spontaneously entered his mind: "Fortunate Son." This time there were no SEALs or GIs in the wings to recover casualties in the Vietnamese jungle, only two civilians who were surveying their surroundings with a serious look. Perhaps they were expecting to come under fire from the local rebels, Kollerup thought. Both made it unnecessarily clear with a military hand signal that they had spotted Kollerup.

The wheels of the helicopter bounced on the well-kept lawn as the passengers jumped out more or less elegantly. Ducking, Lührssen and Eysenhardt hurried out from under the rotors. Kolle wondered why the prosecutor was afraid for his head; even with his arms raised, his hands would have been out of harm's way. Now they could see the completely different clothing the two men were wearing. Eysenhardt in his typical billowing coat, which made the already not-exactly-tall man look even smaller. Next to him the coroner, pathologist and forensic scientist Professor Doctor Lührssen, once again dressed smartly and suitably for the occasion: olive green rubber boots, clothes in a fashionable camouflage pattern, and on his head, a similarly spotted baseball cap. He was also carrying several heavy cases, which apparently contained his work equipment. When they reached the waiting inspector, Lührssen threw his luggage into the grass, cursing, and theatrically wiped the sweat from his forehead with an olive-green handkerchief.

"Moin, Kolle," he groaned as they shook hands. In the meantime, Eysenhardt caught up with them and rumbled a greeting in his baritone. As was his way, his hand disappeared in Napoleonic fashion into his coat flap. His other hand twirled his enormous mustache, which he constantly kept tightly curled. While someone might scratch the back of his neck when embarrassed or put his index finger and thumb on the bridge of his nose, Eysenhardt twirled his mustache.

Kollerup introduced Onne, providing a brief review of his assistance, which he praised.

"I can see, my dear Kollerup, that once again I have the right man on the job!" The prosecutor praised himself for a decision that hadn't even been his to make.

He looked around, rocking on his feet as he did so, as if speculating on where he intended to station his troops.

When the rotor blades finally stopped, the prosecutor asked Kollerup to tell him about what had happened: "Well, bring us up to speed!"

With military brevity, Kolle filled his colleagues in on the events of the past twenty-four hours. Meanwhile, the coroner Lührssen made impatient hand signals in the direction of the hotel and tapped on his watch. Kolle finished and made a clueless gesture.

"It's advisable to perform a detailed autopsy as soon as possible to get an accurate picture of the circumstances of the death," lectured Lührssen with a raised index finger, as if he were in a classroom.

"Well, come with us." Kolle and Onne led the way, neither being generous enough to offer to carry any of the doctor's luggage. When the group of four reached the steps, the two newcomers leaned their heads back, and their eyes widened.

"Man, Kolle! You won this in a competition?" whispered Lührssen in awe.

"What kind of competition was it?" Eysenhardt wanted to know.

Kollerup played the hardened competitor.

"Nothing special, I just had to find a hidden object in a picture. The title was 'Where's the cat?' The first person to find the cat, won."

"You're joking, right?" Onne was horrified. A hidden object!

At the top of the steps, they were greeted by the hotel manager Budnik and his staff.

"Moin! My name is Eysenhardt, and I'm a prosecutor from Husum. And this man here..." he pointed at the panting Lührssen, "is our coroner, pathologist and forensic scientist, Professor Lührssen."

"And obedient pack mule!" the doctor muttered inarticulately as he wiped the sweat from his forehead with another theatrical flourish. Budnik introduced himself and then his colleagues, who were lined up as if at a state reception. "If you would follow me?" Budnik asked, before marching into the foyer. His wife was sitting in the office, and she immediately jumped up when the group entered.

The prosecutor charmingly breathed a kiss onto the hand offered to him and twirled his mustache. Since the arrival of the helicopter had not gone unnoticed—it had made enough noise—it wasn't surprising that all the guests were also present. The patio door was open, and the late afternoon light cast a surreal atmosphere.

"So, ahem..." Eysenhardt cleared his throat before explaining to everyone why the two of them were there. Kollerup rolled his eyes and wondered if he really thought everyone was so simpleminded as to be unaware of why a prosecutor and a pathologist would drop from the sky after a death.

"When can we go home?" The Maybach's son was staring at

the strange man with the funny mustache.

"Well, my boy, we can't do that quite yet. It's not so bad here though, is it?"

"Well, no…" Kurt Sievertsen spoke up now and added, "Nevertheless, some of us have commitments elsewhere."

"Nonsense!" Eysenhardt waved him off. "You have booked several weeks here anyway. Consider it an adventure vacation. Things are better here than on the mainland." That was the end of the matter for him. He went on to report on how things were across the sea. Things were bad but could've been worse, he reassured them. Some injuries, high property damage, part of the population in emergency shelters. Ships could only operate to a limited extent at the moment, and most of the ferry piers were damaged. Towns such as Husum, Dagebüll and Büsum were inaccessible by sea, or only accessible with some difficulty. Those who had relatives on the west coast had to be patient until the telephone connections were available again. Maybe by tomorrow, he assured those present.

Then he clapped his hands and called out, "Well, where is the good gentleman?"

"In the cold storage room, Mr. Prosecutor!" Onne pointed with his thumb toward the kitchen.

"Good fellow! Lead the way! Kolle? Lührssen!"

The three of them stood freezing in the cold room, gazing at the pale figure of the dead man. Lührssen had done what he could and confirmed, raising his voice in high praise, Kolle's findings from his superficial examination. "Death by extensive blood loss due to the wound in the neck. Whether poisons, drugs or other things were involved, of course, we will only know after the final and all-encompassing…"

"Spare us," the prosecutor interjected. "We know that you're the best." Then he pulled out his radio and called for the pilot to come get the body.

Lührssen packed up his things, including the evidence. The

dead man's belongings were placed in a transport container, and less than ten minutes later, the helicopter was in the air.

"Keep me posted on events at the front," Eysenhardt droned in farewell.

When peace had returned to the hallig, the swallows and sparrows emerged from their hiding places, and the guests streamed into the open air. There was nothing useful they could do anyway; at least that was what the stranded told themselves. Kolle looked at his watch and realized it was already evening. The first day after the death. Onne had gone back to be with his sheep. There was still so much to do, and Mr. Onne had gone off to go count his sheep or something! Kolle strolled around the haubarg.

The building was surprisingly sturdy after all, he thought as he glanced up at the massive gable. Near the annex, where the generator was located, Malte was playing with an object that looked remarkably like a gun.

HALLIG
First day after the storm
7:30 p.m.

"HEY, MALTE!" KOLLERUP SHOUTED, RAISING HIS hands as he approached. "Who are you planning on shooting?"

Malte looked at the inspector with one narrowed eye. "Are you a spy?"

"Who wants to know?" growled Kolle.

Malte played along. "I have the gun, so I'll ask the questions. Got it?" He raised the pistol, which looked damn real. Today's small caliber guns weren't particularly heavy, not like a decent .45. The kid could just barely grip it with one hand. It was such a small black thing that it understandably looked like a toy gun. Nowadays, hand guns had hardly any weight and a barely noticeable recoil. No problem for children. And the one Malte was holding was definitely a real gun!

"Before you do that, you should take the safety off. You can't fire it like that," he tried the age-old trick of holding out an open hand to Malte. Visibly irritated, the boy started fiddling with the pistol.

"Give it to me. I will show you how it works. You'll get it back, I promise." His tone grew sterner.

"It's not loaded anyway." Malte shrugged in disappointment and handed it to him. Kolle breathed a sigh of relief once he clicked the safety back in place.

"May I keep it?"

"Sure, I don't care. But my dad will be pretty mad when he sees that you've got his gun!" the brat crowed with pleasure. "Gotta go..." he shouted and sped off toward the hotel.

Unbelievable! Kolle located Mr. Maybach at the damaged jetty, where he was busy separating the trash. The inspector borrowed an e-bike, refused to leave a deposit for the bike rental, and sped off.

"Does this belong to you?" Furious, Kolle tossed the gun onto the loading area of the trailer where damp wood was lying. As he did so, he glanced sharply at Maybach, who hesitated for a moment before nodding guiltily.

"Your papers, right now! Gun license, et cetera!"

"I don't have them on me. They're in the hotel," came the meek answer from the visibly shocked father. He looked up. His face was as white as snow.

"It's not loaded," he muttered.

"You're coming with me now, and we'll check those papers!" Kolle hoisted the bike onto the trailer. "Into the car, now!" he ordered. They drove to the hotel without saying a word.

In Kolle's makeshift office, they sat silently at the table. Kollerup had time on his hands, so he slowly sipped his delicious coffee, which he had ordered from Nele at the bar. He looked out the window. Spectacular view! The golden light was creating an effect through a layer of haze that reminded him of dream sequences in various films he had seen. Every now and then, an electric vehicle raced through the picture. The papers in front of him were all in order. Gun ownership card, gun license, all well and good. Nevertheless, Maybach's careless storing of his firearm was a mystery to him.

Sighing, Kolle looked at his watch and saw that it was after seven. He emptied his coffee cup and stood up. Before leaving the room, he said, "You'll probably face charges for this."

Outside in the hallway, he ran into Onne. "Well, all the sheep accounted for?"

"Yeah."

"I need to go outside and have a smoke."

Behind the haubarg, where the parking spaces for the electric vehicles and the charging stations were located, the guests had started to return. They had obviously had a lot of fun, and looked anything but exhausted as they joked and laughed with each other. One of them had something to hide. Kolle studied them closely. There was the lesbian couple, Franziska Koch and Ilona Schneider. Two different people. Outwardly normal, nice people who fit the general female ideal. Attractive, relatively young and with a sexual charisma that a man could hardly resist. But how far would a man go if he absolutely wanted to have one of these hot women? And how far would Franziska Koch go to fight back? Kolle could see that she would have been physically superior to Wolters. A punch to the face is all it would probably have taken for him to give up. Kolle needed to look through the dossier on the two women again; maybe he had overlooked something.

Then followed the Sievertsens. Today, for once, not in sand-dune gear. Kurt and Heidi looked lost in their oversized overalls from the hotel, but also happy. What did the two have to hide, besides the fact that they were related to the dead man? It was not an official interrogation, but they could have told him.

Christa Hansen drove up with them in the same vehicle. A cool and unapproachable lady. Tall, yet very feminine. A typical northerner. Could she kill a man? If the price was right, anyone could kill. And anyone could be bought. Everybody had a financial inhibition threshold, which could be removed with enough money.

The last individuals in the caravan of guests were Mrs. Maybach and her son. She was inconspicuous, neat and quiet. Most of the time, they were the ones you would never think could do anything like murder. But these types of people were the inscrutable ones. It was conceivable she could have done it.

It is time, he sighed, to end the vacation. He stubbed out his cigarette and clapped his hands.

"Come on, Onne, we have work to do. You are my

official assistant."

"Gladly. Do you want me to play Miss Marple or Dr. Watson?"

"You mean either the know-it-all nag or the good conscience? Mr. Stringer would do for me, Onne."

"That schmuck who never knows what he's doing?"

"No, the attentive helper who thinks for himself for a change."

HOTEL
The day of the storm
3:00 p.m.

THE CONVERSATION HAD GIVEN CHRISTA A LOT TO think about after her unexpected encounter with Kai. How bitter he had become! What dreams they'd had back then! To work for peace and the environment. She herself had become more realistic over the decades, and many things no longer interested her. But at least she didn't live like he did, without a goal, only on her parents' inheritance. Mudflat guide! She couldn't imagine anything more boring than answering annoying questions from irritating tourists in all kinds of weather.

From electrical engineer and revolutionary to mudflat guide. Life takes strange paths.

Her cell phone rang. The number displayed was unfamiliar to her.

"Hansen?"

"Hey, Chris! Kai here."

"Yes?" How had he gotten her number? Had she given it to him? Not that she...

Wolters interrupted her thoughts. "Do you have plans for tonight yet?"

She hesitated. What does he want?

"Actually, I had wanted to stay in this evening." She concealed the fact that she had a business appointment with Maybach.

"Could a bottle of wine change your mind? The two of us drinking romantically among the sheep on a balmy summer night, with a view of the setting sun, talking about old times."

She thought about it. Maybe she did? Inspired by some gut feeling, she said, "Maybe."

"A maybe gives one hope."

She could arrange to chat with Maybach after meeting with Wolters. After all, she was the only one who was interested in what he had to offer. Maybach would just have to be patient for an hour.

"All right. Half an hour after dinner at the golf course."

Wolters sighed, "I'm glad!"

"Yes, see you then." She broke off the conversation. Strange. How had he gotten her number? Thoughtfully, she tapped in a different number. The engineer answered.

"Maybach."

"Hello, Mr. Maybach. Hansen here. I have to postpone our conversation for an hour. Is that a problem?"

"No, not at all!"

"Well then, how about we meet tonight at 10:00 p.m. at the golf course?"

"The best place would be behind the tool shed. We won't be so exposed there."

"As you wish. No problem, Mr. Maybach."

She glanced at her watch. She had enough time to visit the fitness room before dinner. On her way there, she passed the reception desk. On the screens mounted along the wall down there, news was running around the clock, as it was almost everywhere in hotels around the world. No one can escape the flood of information, she thought, amused. An obviously wind-blown reporter in a trench coat with a bright yellow microphone was on one of the screens. In the background, police cars with nervously flickering lights were lined up in front of a group of trees. Probably on a seashore somewhere, she guessed. The North Sea! She knew where the reporter was standing. Years ago, she had been in Newcastle-upon-Tyne for a business appointment. That was where the agitated lady with her microphone was standing. The camera then panned to several houses that were missing their roofs.

The scrolling text left no question unanswered. "Millennium storm destroys parts of Newcastle... damage in the millions... weather forecasters warn it could affect the German coast."

She asked if the sound could be turned up. Since she spoke very good English, she understood every word. A huge storm, not yet classified as a hurricane or a typhoon, seemed to have moved unexpectedly from the North Atlantic toward the North Sea. It was assumed that the high water temperature of the North Sea was fueling its strength. Fortunately, it was a leftward-rotating depression, otherwise the entire English North Sea coast would have been affected by a severe storm surge. So far, the damage was mostly limited to property. One person had been killed when the rotor hub of a wind turbine had fallen with its blades onto the car in which a maintenance technician had been driving. This had then resulted in a complete power outage in the Newcastle area. All very speculative, of course, she thought. Turbine failures didn't tend to cause power outages. Unless there was a high-voltage line right nearby, which could have been hit by falling parts. Too many unanswered questions, she decided. But the news broadcasters always cared little about the facts. The main thing was to evoke "suspense and thrills." Shaking her head, she thought of the many "facts" cited by opponents of wind power. Of course, something like this would be welcomed with open arms by them. Now the news switched to another area of devastation. She knew this town well, too—Harwich, south of Newcastle. Overturned trucks were shown at the ferry pier. According to the commentary, all continental ferry services had been discontinued, and the damage to the piers was estimated in the millions.

She turned away, tired of the sensationalistic stridency of the reporting. At the exit doors, guests were gathering to check out in order to catch the last ferry to the mainland.

There was a slight hysteria in the air, and the young lady at the reception desk was having a hard time, though she was managing her task professionally, Christa thought. Suddenly, she no longer felt like working out, so she decided to watch the hustle and bustle down at the pier instead.

In front of the hotel, there was no sign of an impending storm. Blue sky, a light breeze and very warm. Only in the west, the haze seemed to be denser than usual. All the available vehicles were flitting around like ants on the only road to the jetty—rush hour on the hallig. Too much hustle and bustle, she decided, and chose to take the path to the church.

She took a deep breath and enjoyed the tense atmosphere. Would her appointments with Wolters and Maybach be affected?

In the sheep meadow, the shepherd was scurrying around and rounding up his flock quite skillfully, in her opinion. Like obedient school children, they let themselves be driven to the church. But also just like children, some always strayed or suddenly discovered something terribly exciting to investigate.

She remembered the name of the shepherd: Onne. An artistic shepherd slapping gloomy motifs onto canvases. He had more mundane things to take care of at the moment. He was apparently driving his flock to the church, which hadn't been used for ten years.

Now it was a sturdy sheepfold. A great many sheep were still coming to the former place of worship, so it seemed. Probably it had never been so full even back when the hallig was still populated by locals.

But she could also see that her meeting with Kai wouldn't work out. A rendezvous between sheep might be totally romantic for some, but for Christa, who had grown up with sheep, it would be an absolute nightmare.

She briefly considered canceling both meetings on short notice, but wondered if she could find a new place just as spontaneously.

At the helipad, she turned around and followed a side path that led back to the hotel behind the miniature golf course. The path brought her close to the building where the employees lodged.

From a distance, she spotted Kai creeping toward the lodge with his head down. She suppressed the impulse to call out a greeting to him. Even days later, she couldn't say exactly why she didn't. It looked as if he was carrying heavy thoughts with him, so she left him to his worries and went to the hotel.

It was surprisingly quiet in the foyer. All the day guests had taken the last ferry out.

The news on television was now dominated by the storm. A meteorologist was waxing eloquent about what might happen, when this or that might arrive, and what the consequences might be.

Typical sensationalist journalism, thought Christa. As if what happened wasn't terrible enough. Always adding to it to keep consumers hooked. She asked the receptionist to turn up the volume.

"...when the above factors come together, the same situation could arise as we've seen before. You remember? On July 30, 2010, one of the largest hurricanes since weather records have been kept hit the offshore island of Helgoland. A few days earlier, the island of Sylt was affected. Islanders still remember the extensive casualties and damage that storm caused."

Amateur pictures and shaky videos followed, showing an ominous cloud rotating toward the Helgoland dunes.

"If temperatures remain this high, it is possible that the hurricane that struck the British North Sea coast could grow larger as it moves westward. This, in turn, could result in widespread damage to the coast."

Now a map of the west coast of Schleswig-Holstein was displayed. Areas marked in red showed where the storm could unleash its greatest destruction. The entire coast was red, including the halligs and the islands in the Wadden Sea.

"The greatest danger is the potential," the meteorologist explained, "for several small hurricanes to merge into one large one."

The graphic changed again, with the red area now covering the whole of Schleswig-Holstein.

"But this is really the most unlikely case." He grinned into the camera and waved his hands placatingly.

Christa had seen enough and shook her head. Scaremongering reports like this were enough to make you pull out your hair. The presenter pointed out that a severe weather warning had been issued for the coming night. He warned campers to cancel planned barbecues and to take down their tents as a precaution. The broadcast was then interrupted by a commercial for stormproof umbrellas. Christa laughed out loud. Unbelievable! Umbrellas in a hurricane!

In the restaurant area, cutlery and dishes were being eagerly rattled. In the hotel, everything seemed to be running as usual. The employees, who obviously had a good relationship with each other, were joking and laughing together. The smells of roasted meat and spices drifted through the first floor, as the cook's orders to his assistants emanated from the kitchen.

She was hungry now. While she was changing, she briefly considered canceling her appointments. What if things turned out as the hysterical news suggested? Pfft! The news was supposed to report, not assume! She snorted disdainfully. As a north German girl, she already had numerous storms under her belt, the kind you could lean into without falling over. A small waterspout didn't frighten her. So she left her appointments as they were.

Dressed in evening attire, she walked out to the back entrance to admire the sunset. Her heart stopped in shock when she saw the black wall approaching from the west. Wow!

The hotel technician, who was leaving the generator shed just at that moment, nodded at her.

"Moin."

"Moin," she returned the greeting.

"It won't be all that bad!" The technician jerked his thumb at the wall of clouds. She waved it off.

"That's not as bad as what I'm used to. I'm from here."

Then they made small talk about old times and past storms.

"Well, then... I have to get back to work and close up all the bulkheads and stuff."

She raised her hand in farewell, as one does on the coast when one calls out "Take care!" to say goodbye.

It was growing noticeably cooler, and a stiff breeze tugged at her hair. Prudently, she shut the door as she entered the haubarg. She knew what could happen with open doors and windows in a strong wind.

She ordered her food and glanced around the restaurant. Surprisingly, not all the hotel guests had fled the rumored storm. She was seated in front of the window facing the terrace, where she could enjoy the magnificent panorama as if in front of a big screen. The black wall rushed toward her. The first violent gusts of wind made the small bar outside shake, as the wind drove forgotten napkins past her view. The sun had long since been swallowed up by the cloud front, and it was now getting so dark that the outside lights had automatically switched on.

When her first course arrived, the rain began to fall outside, followed shortly by hail. The barrage lasted less than five minutes, at which point the hail turned into rain, which seemed to want to flood the hallig. Then a flash of lightning. She began to count as she had learned in school. Two seconds later, the thunder rumbled, and the haubarg went dark. A woman shrieked hysterically.

Budnik, the owner of the Deichvogt, spoke a few soothing words, and then the lights came back on. It grew dark again when she reached for the water glass. A second later, a pale figure was illuminated by a flash of lightning. Kai!

As if in slow motion, she watched the scene unfold. With a grimace and his bloody hands against the window, he stared at her!

She noticed that, oddly enough, he wasn't wearing rain gear, only a light jacket. And an irrational concern for his health seized her. In the next flash, which illuminated the macabre stage shortly after the first flash, Wolters lay motionless on the terrace.

She knew instantly that any help she could offer would be too late.

HOTEL
First day after the storm
8:00 p.m.

WITH ALL THE GUESTS GATHERED, THIS WAS THE ideal opportunity to make a straightforward speech about the fact he was now officially in charge of the case. Getting to his feet, he was about to announce that he was now - when he was interrupted by Budnik. Kollerup rolled his eyes and hoped silently that this wouldn't become a habit.

"Inspector! Telephone! It's important."

It was Lührssen. Apparently, he and his assistant had been working overtime.

"My dear Kolle, you've made a big mistake! So much for it being an accident."

Kollerup had played this game for years! Any second now, he would prod his colleague to ask what he meant, what he'd found.

"What do you think I found? Well? Guess, guess!"

"Your mind, which you lost last week?

"Oh, Kolle! Be serious for once!"

"They found a dead alien in the corpse, which burrowed into Wolters' chest during the storm!"

After taking a loud breath on the other end of the line, Lührssen fired off the next question: "Is that supposed to be funny?"

"You started it!"

"Well, almost. You're close."

"Shot? No, that I would've seen. Any other external possibilities as well. So either poison or -" He was interrupted, which he had been expecting.

"Well, then, it looks like your high school diploma and police training weren't in vain after all. You guessed right. Poison. Now it's up to you to figure out whether he took it voluntarily, or ... you know what I mean."

"What kind of poison?"

"A sleeping pill and .3 blood alcohol level. It's a small miracle the dead man could even walk upright at all, nevermind in the storm on top of it! All the right ingredients for a fatal accident. However, now it's your turn. I'll send you the report right now. Is your internet working again?"

Kolle asked Budnik before replying. "Yes, but it's really slow."

"Alright, I'll send it to you as an email. You have time on your hands!" Lührssen chuckled.

"Is that supposed to be funny?" Kolle repeated Lührssen's earlier question and hung up.

Back in the restaurant, the guests looked at him expectantly.

"I'm sorry, folks!" he raised both hands placatingly. "I ask for your understanding now that our relaxed time is over. Although the connections to the mainland have been severed and it is unlikely that any of you will leave the island, I must point out that, from this point forward, no one is allowed to leave the hallig. No one." At this, he glanced at Budnik and, addressing him, said, "You're responsible for ensuring that your employees follow my instructions." Addressing the guests, he said, "The call just now—" pausing for effect, he took a sip of water and continued, "—came from the coroner, who is also a pathologist. Guess what he told me?"

Kolle thought he was doing great! Filling them with uncertainty by giving them only partial knowledge. Some of the guests were becoming visibly nervous. The Sievertsen couple held each other's hands tensely. Maybach turned pale. Most of them just shrugged in response to his question.

"I don't want to keep you in suspense." Kolle took another sip of water. He could have read from the phone book or recited recipes from a cookbook. Either way, he had their full attention now. In a conversational tone—as if he were making casual smalltalk such as "By the way, you've got something on your nose"—he declared, "Wolters was pumped full of a narcotic and was three sheets to the wind. We're no longer dealing with an accident, but with a deliberate death. At least, one that was hurried along." Zing! That hit home. "My job is to determine whether suicide or foul play was involved."

He sat down.

The room was as quiet as a cemetary, and even in the otherwise bustling kitchen, the staff stared wordlessly at each other.

"Well, now I'm hungry!" piped up Onne into the dead silence.

Schneider and Koch giggled, breaking the tension, even though giggling wasn't particularly appropriate at the moment.

They were down to two fixed menus to choose from; Budnik had discovered when checking their supplies that they needed to cut their offerings back a bit. Supplies weren't running low yet, but he had to calculate two weeks as a safety buffer. He had reckoned with having more guests, which they would have had if the storm hadn't hit. Thus, the warehouses and cold storage were were full to bursting, but he didn't want to take any risks.

Those present were reasonable, and no one grumbled. After all, they had more than enough of everything. Therefore, the restriction to two menus, both with three courses, was more of a funny punchline than something to be upset about.

Budnik explained that the restrictions would also extend to breakfast, which wouldn't include scrambled eggs and matje herring moving forward. The guests seemed willing to live without them too. Very few ate scrambled eggs or fish for breakfast, and herring wasn't good breakfast food anyway, in Kollerup's opinion.

So on the first evening after the storm, there was a choice of a vegetarian meal or one with meat.

When everyone was full and tired after the eventful day, they settled into the available armchairs, while the hotel owner offered each of them a drink of their choice.

At this point, the evening grew interesting, and the group became noticeably closer.

The dominant topic was the storm, while the death wasn't mentioned at all. Each of the guests had experienced storms and hurricanes in their lifetimes, at least once if not more often. Heidi and Kurt Sievertsen shared several humorous experiences they'd had on Föhr during the hurricanes of the last few decades. Then, suddenly, everyone else had a story to tell. In the process, Onne turned out to be an eloquent entertainer and creative storyteller. His stories were peppered with witty punchlines, which were accompanied by much laughter. Kolle wasn't a great orator, but he was at least as creative when he told stories about his cats, who freaked out at the sound of storms. Franziska and Ilona were relaxed, and did nothing to conceal their romantic relationship. It was almost like a family Christmas.

Onne was of the opinion that everyone present, having been brought together by fate, should consider themselves on a first-name basis. This was met with general approval, and everyone offered their first names. Kolle did too, although he didn't think the pressure to use familiar names was warranted. People knew best for themselves whom they wanted to be on first- or last-name terms with. However, he didn't want to be a killjoy. Besides, he thought it might be quite helpful in his investigations if there was a certain comradery among the suspects.

During the second round of drinks, someone shouted exuberantly that the employees shouldn't be forgotten. After all, they had all contributed today toward bringing the hallig back into shape. With exuberant bellows, the five men and two women were summoned. The two Budniks also sat down with the group and introduced themselves. Bernd and Helga were their first names. Bernd was a typical North German manager. On the one hand, he was friendly, but always a little distant. His usual condescending joviality disappeared after a gin and tonic, and the man who emerged proved to be a rather modest person. Helga was the hands-on type and maternal.

They, too, had one or two stories to tell, mildly amusing ones to the tune of "a married couple tells a joke." Each one tried to one up the other's comments with things like "Honey, you're not telling it quite right." The result was a chaotic story, which the audience rewarded with much applause.

In the meantime, the staff had also been supplied with drinks and were sitting among the guests. You could feel everyone relaxing, and the lounge music in the background did the rest to create a special atmosphere.

The kitchen produced a small snack for those gathered, and Arne, the assistant to Thore, the cook, explained eloquently and with a wink what delicacies lay on the silver trays. Most of it was composed of canned fish, but the goodies were prepared in such a way as to mask their canned origin. There was a lot of eating, and etiquette expectations for how one should behave at a buffet were ignored.

Then the landline in the office rang. With an apologetic look around, Bernd Budnik trotted off, only to return less than a minute later. Kolle could tell from a distance that it was an important call. A cop was never off-duty. It was Larsson. Kollerup fleetingly wondered what his first name was. Seigur or something. An Icelandic name as he remembered.

"What's up?"

"Work."

"Thanks. Got some already."

"How about some more?"

"Thanks, I've got enough already."

"Eysenhardt is sending the forensics team out to you around nine tomorrow."

"His foot soldiers?"

"Always when it's murder."

"What do you mean murder?"

"Lührssen's final report..."

"Why am I only finding out about this now?"

"It was emailed to you earlier, Chief!"

"Oh, okay. Yes, I got it, but I haven't read it yet."

"He wanted me to tell you about it. He has more important things to do now."

"Good, thank you. Good night, Seigur."

"Good night, Chief."

MINIATURE GOLF COURSE
The day of the storm
4:00 p.m.

FRANK PEERED AT THE BALL AT THE END OF HIS golf club. Yes, this should work. He rose from his crouch and positioned himself above the ball. The rest of the family watched in boredom. Marianne wanted to go to the beach, and Malte just thought the game was stupid. His father always made a big fuss when he won, which was a rarity, because Malte was a natural at miniature golf and usually won with a lead of at least ten points.

But his father was an engineer! Everything had to be calculated. Despite carefully aiming and taking his two shots, his father often had the misfortune that the ball insisted on doing what it wanted. And that was the case now. With a crack, whop, and kathunk, it landed on the trail.

"Dad, don't hit it so hard!"

"I don't get it. According to my calculations, the ball should've gone in."

"Dad, watch." He set his ball on the tee and, without hesitation, hit it down the zigzag path. With a clack-clack-clack, it landed in the hole. Sometimes he suspected that his father was letting him win on purpose. It was so easy, after all!

Frank Maybach's phone rang.

"Sorry, but do I have to... Maybach!... No. Not at all!... Well, the best place is behind the tool shed. Not so exposed."

Marianne looked at him.

"It's Hansen. Tonight at ten here at the golf course."

"I'll be glad when the deal is finally over," his wife sighed.

"Me, too, sweetheart. Me, too. So... champ, how about a break? Ice cream?"

"A coke!" shouted Malte. However, all he got was mineral water.

Afterwards, they planned to take part in a mudflat hike before dinner, as the tide was going out. Only after they had finished changing and had prepared themselves appropriately—which involved Malte's mother insisting that he put on sunscreen with a SPF of 50—did they learn that the mudflat hike had been canceled because of the impending storm. Frank complained immediately at the front desk, because there was absolutely no sign of the storm in the sky! But Mrs. Budnik was adamant. She referred to the weather warning and insisted that she, as the organizer, couldn't be responsible for exposing the participants to any storm-related risks. Frank was horrified! He wanted to meet with Wolters today. His deal was in jeopardy! What would happen if they couldn't get together at all because of the weather? Fortunately he still had Hansen as an additional card up his sleeve. If everything fell through because of the weather, he was at a dead end. The long preparations, his carefully laid plans would then have been in vain. This was a once-in-a-lifetime opportunity. He was devastated.

Malte was ticked off! Here he stood, as greased and slippery as a sausage in frying oil, with no exciting hike to the sunken Rungholt settlement in the works! When his mother suggested to him that they could go to the beach to fly the kite he had brought with him, he simply said, "Nope."

Then he went back to their room to wash off the stupid

grease. He took a long shower, which wasn't so bad considering how much fun he could have talking to it. What all she knew! When he started to argue with her about the connection between light water and heavy water, his parents came and ended the dispute.

His father seemed to be in a foul mood, while his mother was even more taciturn than usual.

"I'll try to call Wolters. Maybe things aren't as bad as I think." Frank Maybach threw himself backward onto the bed.

Marianne, who was in the bathroom with Malte, heard indistinctly that Frank was apparently in luck when Wolters picked up. After a few minutes, her husband called out that he was going to meet Wolters now. Stepping into the bathroom, he said, "Wolters is on the island. He thinks that now is the best time to meet. I'm going to head off. It shouldn't take more than half an hour."

"Don't forget," his wife reminded him anxiously, "that supper's in an hour. Are you taking a raincoat with you? You know... the storm."

"Oh, no worries. I'll be back by then!"

"Call me if anything comes up."

"What could possibly go wrong?"

"Oh, I just have a feeling..." She left the sentence hanging.

He winked at her and disappeared.

Shortly before the promised half hour had elapsed, Frank returned, grinning. "All right. I gave him a set of copies, and he seemed interested. The man's not so dim, either."

Marianne smiled. "Wonderful! And what did he say?"

"He said he'd look into it, and will let me know the day after tomorrow what his company thinks of it. He's an electrical engineer, by the way. Studied in Münster."

"Then we can celebrate a partial success today," his wife declared joyfully.

Malte, who was watching his favorite movie, *Dr. Who and the Mystery of the Nautilus*, called out from the background: "Yay! And I'll celebrate with a giant glass of gin!"

Dr. Who was a passionate gin drinker. Malte knew full well that only adults were allowed to drink alcohol, but it couldn't hurt to try.

"Sure, partner!" called Frank, pinching his upper arm.

"Now please get ready for dinner," his wife reminded him. It was getting dark outside.

"Well... we should get on with this, before the world ends," Frank joked. He was in boisterous spirits, fully convinced that he could close the deal within a week. And he still had Christa Hansen, his trump card, up his sleeve.

Whistling and joking with Malte, he dashed down the stairs. Marianne was delighted! At last, her husband was getting the recognition he deserved.

Their happiness came to an abrupt end when Wolters collapsed dead at the patio door.

HOTEL
First day after the storm
10:00 p.m.

AFTER THE PHONE CALL, THE LEISURELY END OF THE first "day after" lost some of its relaxed vibes. The laughter was no longer so boisterous, and the people moved a little farther apart. With the pathologist's report across his knees, Kollerup no longer belonged to the circle of revelers. He didn't care though, because what the final report contained was much more exciting. This was the very reason Prosecutor Eysenhardt had pressed for a forensics team to be reassigned from somewhere else and sent off to Grienoog as quickly as possible.

They were to arrive early tomorrow morning. "Around nine o'clock," as his colleague Larsson had told him.

Thus, it came as no surprise to anyone when the inspector decided to withdraw before midnight in order to consult with Onne.

"According to the report, we're now dealing with an intentional death."

"A murder, Kolle?"

"No, Onne. I'm not a lawyer, but at the very least, negligent bodily injury resulting in death. In the past, these kinds of cases were treated as murder."

"Well... dead is dead. Poisoned, shot or whatever."

"Not quite. You have to consider intent and attempt to

harm. And don't forget about crimes of passion. Well... and lots more. Motive is also important."

Kolle didn't really care about the sentence a judge would hand down. He wanted to solve the case. Who was the culprit, and why and how had they done it? That was it, quite simple actually.

Over the next half hour, he explained to his assistant what was in the report: Wolters had been poisoned with a cocktail consisting of two different substances. One was an antihistamine, which was also a highly effective sleeping pill. The other substance was ricin, which is contained in the seed of the miracle tree. When combined with alcohol, this drug cocktail wouldn't lead to immediate death, but to a state close to it. Wolters would have died sooner or later from the continuous administration of ricin, which he must have been given in small doses over a longer period of time. The poison had basically led to minor internal bleeding.

"So, if you wanted to kill someone with this stuff, you'd need to lay the groundwork ahead of time. Logically, this can't be a crime of passion. Unless Wolters himself took the overdose of sleeping pills, and the other poison was more of an encore."

Onne considered this for a few moments before replying. "That means there could be two culprits."

"Or just one," Kolle objected.

"The question, then," Onne pondered aloud, "is in what order did the poisons enter the body."

"Exactly! What bothers me is, on the one hand, the high blood loss. On the other hand, the internal bleeding could be explained by the ricin." Kolle gave this some thought.

Bernd had already given him the site map for the staff lodge, since they were now on a first-name basis. But logically every hotel had several such maps, otherwise the rooms couldn't be cleaned and tidied up. Like the hotel, the doors on the employees' rooms were equipped with card readers that could lock and unlock them. So there was a danger that anyone with a master room card could easily remove incriminating evidence.

"Have you already been in Wolters' room to look for the safe?" asked Kollerup abruptly.

"Nah, haven't had time yet."

"We have to make up for what we've missed so far. Wolters' room needs to be sealed."

"How?" Onne was at a loss.

"Quite simple. All it takes is a scrap of paper or a match."

They made their way, unnoticed, to the employee's lodge. Once there, Kolle prepared the door; he had seen this before in spy films.

He stuck a match in the lower area between the door and the door frame and broke it off. If someone were to open the door, the broken part would fall to the floor. No one ever paid attention to matches, not even intruders.

Onne was delighted. "Kolle, you're good!" he exclaimed excitedly.

The flattered man waved this off. "You should see what I can make with a bubble gum wrapper, a battery, and matches."

"A bomb?" His assistant was in seventh MacGyver heaven.

"Maybe. But you're impressed, aren't you?"

"Show-off!"

Kolle was suddenly weary. "It's time for me to go to bed. We have to be bright-eyed and bushy-tailed tomorrow. "

Onne, on the other hand, wanted to rejoin the guests and just have a nightcap.

HOTEL
The day of the storm
11:00 a.m.

TODAY THEY SLEPT IN LONG. WHEN ILONA GOT UP, she complained about her sore muscles as she crawled laboriously out of bed. Franziska, who had already finished showering and dressing, was obviously none the worse for wear.

"If you'd exercise more...." She let the sentence hang in the air. How often had she urged Ilona to go to the gym for strength training? A lot. But she had a soft heart.

"Then you should take a hot shower, my dear."

While Ilona crawled to the shower, Franziska pulled out her phone. When she was sure that the sound of the water would drown out their conversation, she called Wolters.

"Hello, Mr. Wolters," she breathed seductively, after someone answered with a grim, "Hello?"

"This is Franziska. I wanted to tell you that we've thought it over. Wouldn't it be nice if today we..."

"I can't today!"

"What?" Now she was playing the disappointed mistress. "I thought you'd be happy to get together with us. By the way, I brought along my thong bikini. Would you like me to model it for you tonight?"

"Yes. Uh. Let's see... I'll check my calendar... so today I'm giving a guided tour of the tidal flats—early evening as the tide's going out. After that, maybe? After dark? Say, around eleven?"

"Eleven? Sure, that's when it's most beautiful in the old church! Ilona thinks so too, by the way. She is standing freshly showered in front of me. You should see her now!"

"Uh, it looks like I might be able to meet a little earlier. Before that, I have a business appointment that I can cut short."

"That's awfully nice! I'll bring the drinks. It'll be cozy, won't it?" I have to be careful not to lay it on too thick, she reminded herself. Make him a little hot and bothered, nothing more.

"I think we'll have a... nice time together." His voice quivered a little. She had him now!

"Well, see you then. We're really looking forward to it," she breathed. Then she hung up without saying goodbye. She thrust her fist triumphantly in the air. Yes!

Ilona was still in the bathroom. Why do women always take so long in there? Anyway, this gave her the opportunity to put the special drink in the fridge. She had also thought of plastic glasses, which could be disposed of afterward without any problems. As soon as she'd gotten everything ready, Ilona stepped out of the bathroom freshly made up.

"Hey, are you finally ready?" asked Franziska with a wink.

On her way into the bathroom, she gave Ilona a slap on her sweet rear, which the latter perkily thrust toward her.

After breakfast, they strolled to the pier and sat down on the wooden planks. "I spoke to Wolters earlier on the phone," Franziska informed her partner. "You should wear your short dress, the red one with the lacy top."

"Just the dress?" asked Ilona with a twinkle in her eye.

"Just the dress," she confirmed.

"Okaaaaaay." Ilona drew out the last syllable meaningfully.

Franziska went over the details with her, as she kept an eye on what was going on around them. After all, you never knew who might be close enough to overhear them. The day guests were all either on the beach or in the bar. One or the other was whizzing around on one of the e-bikes. The next ferry wasn't expected until the afternoon, so they could discuss their plan undisturbed.

The waves lapped sluggishly against the rock-strewn embankment, while swallows sailed at breakneck speed through the heat. A brilliant blue sky arched over the Wadden Sea mudflats. And two women continued their plotting on how to make a man disappear without a trace.

By noon, the plan was perfect, there was nothing more to say. Hand in hand, two women dressed in summer clothing silently made their way back to the haubarg. They changed into something slightly less conspicuous for lunch.

At the outside bar sat a man, completely out of place in black jeans and a black shirt, a braid dangling down his back. Ilona wrinkled her cute nose at the strange guy, who was chatting with the bartender and sipping on a long drink. Probably a day guest, she thought, who didn't feel like walking around in the scorching heat. His wife and children were probably at the beach, and Daddy was waiting until he could go home.

The two women sat down at one of the tables and ordered a light lunch. As they ate in silence, they heard the front desk getting noisy, but this didn't bother them. It was none of their business.

The guy from the bar got up and walked past their table, without paying any attention to them. Weird guy, Franziska thought. Anyone else would have stared at her.

After lunch, they stretched out on one of the loungers on the artificial beach. Umbrellas provided enough shade for them to doze off occasionally without risk of burning, while watching the hustle and bustle of the day guests. Lulled by the sleepy lounge music, they didn't notice how the beach was emptying. Mothers grabbed their whining children and hurriedly left the bathing area.

Only once it grew noticeably cooler did they open their

eyes. Far off on the horizon, they could see a black line. A light wind blew up, making them shiver. Only then did they realize that they were the only ones on the beach. All the beach and deckchairs were empty, and the bartender had put away his drinks and bar utensils. Inside the restaurant, the tables were being set for dinner.

Life on vacation seemed to consist solely of eating and sleeping. One hardly finished breakfast before it was time to sit down again for lunch. Franziska enjoyed this rhythm, but she knew Ilona didn't care one way or the other. Their day-to-day routine was exhausting enough as it was, so her motto was to never rush around when on vacation.

Besides, they were scheduled to have a good time tonight. She was seriously looking forward to giving her life a new perspective. Ilona was only along because she trusted her blindly.

Now it was getting considerably cooler. "Come on, let's go and change for dinner," she urged Ilona.

At supper, they ran into the black-clad guy for the second time. He was dressed inappropriately in his leather jacket, but at least he had showered. You could smell it. Once again, he didn't seem to notice her. However, he glanced several times at a lady who was sitting at the window.

Obviously, the hotel guests were the only ones here this evening. That suited Franziska and Ilona just fine; there would be fewer potential witnesses. They both ordered the crab casserole with a salad. As they were eating dessert, the lights went out. Power failure.

When Franziska saw her evening's date collapse outside, her only thought was that someone had been kind enough to do their dirty work for them.

HOTEL
Second Day After the Storm
9 a.m.

THE MORNING AFTER THE SMALL CELEBRATION, A taciturn Onne sat next to an equally taciturn Husum inspector as he sipped his coffee. While the painter-shepherd was suffering from a hangover to the extent that every loud noise made him wince, Kolle's reluctance to talk had a different motivation. He was concentrating on his work. The various things that had to be done today were swirling around in his head.

The first matter involved the colleagues from the forensics department and the technicians from the laboratory, who were about to arrive. That would be followed by the usual marathon interrogation. Onne could certainly take some things off his hands, but he had to handle the interrogations and conversations personally. He was thinking specifically of the Koch and Schneider couple, as well as the Sieverstens. Maybach played more of a peripheral role, as did his wife.

Christa Hansen was an exception—a slick and diplomatic genius in her field. Such people often weren't above climbing over a mound of dead bodies en route to a lucrative contract. At the top of his list was the Sieversten couple, in second place Ms. Hanson, and at the bottom Maybach and the lesbian couple. From experience, he knew that this list could change at any moment.

Lührssen had mentioned in his report that the poisonous

mixture must have been administered about one to two hours before the death occurred. So late afternoon or early evening, Kolle concluded.

Who'd had motive and opportunity, as well as access to the poison? Getting hold of ricin was simple enough. Every online store sold the seeds; a ten-pack for three euros would be enough to kill a child. The problem was the administration. Perhaps the order could be traced to the perpetrator. Kolle immediately jotted down these thoughts in his tablet.

"You're hooked on games too." Onne was obviously halfway back among the living, and he was peering at the display with interest.

"No. Working. This thing helps sort out my thoughts without loose pages flying around everywhere. And I don't have to keep begging everyone for a pen or a piece of paper."

Kolle had to grin at these thoughts. So many of the crime novels he remembered from the eighties and nineties involved policemen who either broke their pencils or forgot their notepads back at the office. This was certainly an aid when it came to winnowing out suspects. The helpless policeman was more likely to be trusted than the dashing cop who never asked for assistance.

Today there were other ways of building a rapport with suspects.

He filled Onne in on his thoughts regarding the crime.

"A garden at the hotel? Yes. But it's more like a cottage garden with hollyhocks and flowering perennials."

"I can always check. The important thing is the interrogations. You could assist me."

"Yes, boss."

"We need the camera and the microphone."

"I'm on it."

"It's almost nine o'clock. We'll go to the landing site and wait for the infantry."

"The infant? Do you mean his Majesty, the Prince? Or are there children coming?"

"Yes, something like that. They all wear the same romper suits and play Navy CIS."

As the guests, visibly battered and red-eyed, dragged themselves to their chairs, Kolle greeted everyone by their first names. Franziska and Ilona still looked quite fresh, while Kurt and Heidi were obviously the worse for wear. The Maybach family and Christa took their time in showing up. Once they were assembled, Kolle chatted about the evening and then glanced theatrically at his watch.

"Good grief, I have to run!" he cried, overly startled. "See you later!"

Kolle bid the group farewell.

The newcomers arrived with two helicopters and fourteen specialists who were absolute experts in their fields.

What transpired next went down as a first-class action. The Bundeswehr helicopters touched down side by side at the exact same second. As soon as they settled on the ground, the doors flew open and eight men and seven women jumped out of the machines. Crates were unloaded and stacked beside the helicopter pad. This took a total of ten minutes, then the aircraft took off and disappeared in an elegant arc towards the mainland.

Onne was thrilled, though Kollerup was acquainted with such showy exhibitions for the press. The head of the white-clad troops was a buddy of Kolle's, Thore Cartensen: tall, stout, and equipped with a paunch that he proudly pushed in front of him. They had known each other since their time at the police academy. Kolle had remained a police officer, while Thore had embarked on a career as a forensics officer. Now Cartensen was the head of the forensics department. Even though he didn't feel the need to dig around at most crime scenes, he made it a point to be on site for the particularly alluring crimes. This seemed like one such case for him.

They shook hands without saying a word, and Kollrup introduced Onne as his assistant. Then he acquainted Thore with the crime scene. The team leader called his people together, explained the situation, and divided them up. Before they could get to work, though, they had to set up a temporary headquarters. Thore also had a crucial piece of paper with him: a search warrant for the hallig. Kolle could not believe his eyes: for an entire hallig. But that was only logical, since all the buildings belonged to Budnik and thus the hallig was privately owned.

After a brief inspection of the hotel's main rooms, they decided to use the gym. A functional field laboratory was set up so that the initial results could be accurately ascertained on site.

When everything was as it should be, a briefing was held in which the team members were assigned their responsibilities. Six officers were tasked with searching the rooms, four were sent to the church, and another four were given the staff lodge.

"Now then! The evidence awaits!" Thore shouted and clapped his hands.

Thore and Kolle went together with their small delegation to the employees' lodge. Standing in front of the door of the apartment where the dead man had lived, they slipped into coveralls. Kolle checked his improvised seal. No one had entered the room. They opened the door and stepped inside a world that took them completely unawares.

HOTEL
The Day of the Storm
10 a.m.

KURT AND HEIDI SPENT THE MORNING PREPARING for the day's tasks. They planned to participate in the mudflat hike that afternoon and to start convincing Wolters to meet with them the next week. They were going to take their time, so that the measures they had plotted against him could have a profound effect. The goal was to destroy him as he had destroyed their daughter. But there wasn't to be even a slight hint as to their involvement in what happened next. Their revenge had to be perfect.

After lunch they took an afternoon nap, as they had been doing since they'd retired. Half an hour of dozing, of resting their eyes. As they stared at the ceiling, they held hands. And then came the memories.

At the time, they had still been living in Mildstedt near Husum. Their daughter had been biking home from a friend's house that night in November, and it had happened on a curve. A car had hit her and thrown the girl into a ditch. She'd died instantly, as the emergency doctor had later assured her parents.

Years later, they'd learned that Wolters must have been responsible. At a mutual relative's wedding reception, Kai had talked about a drunken night he had spent in some music club. He had naturally offered to drive everyone home that evening. On the way, he had briefly lost control of the car and landed in a ditch. He and his friends had pushed the car back onto the street before driving off again. They apparently never noticed that they had killed someone.

The Sieverstens had politely inquired and learned that everything matched: the day, the time, and the place of the accident.

Kai Wolters had killed their daughter.

They'd set an alarm as they always did, but they'd fallen into a deep sleep and didn't hear the alarm. Later than planned—it was already early afternoon—Kurt startled awake and woke Heidi. After a short pause for reflection, they changed for the mudflat hike.

They were having a coffee at the bar when they learned that the tour had been cancelled. Perplexed, they stood in the midst of the hustle and bustle of the departing guests and didn't know what to do. Should they also leave?

The television, which hung on the wall behind the reception desk, was tuned to a channel that ran the latest news. A storm was coming. There was apparently considerable damage in Britain from a whirlwind of unforeseen scale. Now it was on its way across the North Sea, heading straight toward the west coast of Schleswig-Holstein. Kurt couldn't believe all the excitement over a petty summer storm.

Pictures of destroyed wharves and ships that had been tossed onto their piers followed, before moving on to houses with missing roofs and collapsed wooden buildings. If he hadn't known it was the English coast, he would have thought this footage was from Texas or one of the southern Gulf Coast states. These pictures were practically identical to those shown whenever a hurricane passed over the US, but this time it was right on Europe's doorstep.

Kurt and Heidi were now at a loss as to how to proceed.

"Maybe it would be best to postpone the whole thing until next week," Kurt declared in resignation.

Heidi nodded in agreement and said, "He's not running away from us."

When they stepped outside the door of the hotel, they caught sight of Wolters, who at this moment was walking toward the staff lodge. That's true, Heidi thought, he's not running away from us.

They decided to lounge a bit on the beach and wait for dinner. They still had four or five hours until the evening—an opportunity to read a good book. They entered the haubarg through the back door, and as they passed the gym, they overheard an argument. Apparently, it was about a relationship.

An angry female voice snarled, "That pig! I'll make him pay for this!"

"What will you do, Nele? Sue him? He's laughing at you," answered a male voice.

"I know, Jan-Ole. I've already thought of something. If he refuses, I'll tell anyone who'll listen! They should know what kind of person he is."

"When were you going to meet with him?"

"After dinner, but he called me, and said he didn't have time and wanted to discuss all this tomorrow. But I have to do it today, or I'll go crazy if I don't! Why I got involved with Wolters is a mystery to me now. I was so blind! "

"Maybe I should...?"

"No! I have to do this alone."

"But I can help you!"

"No, I don't want to involve you in this."

"Nele, whatever you have planned, I'll stand by you."

After a pause, they heard Nele again.

"Well then... I don't know... it would be best if he disappeared completely. You could help me throw him into the water. The tide will take care of the rest."

"That's what we'll do," replied Jan-Ole. "Call me when you go to him."

"We should go back up front, otherwise the others will notice."

Kurt and Heidi moved off, and not a moment too soon! When they reached the stairs to the second floor, Jan-Ole and Nele left the haubarg through the back entrance.

Kurt whispered to Heidi, "Did you hear that? Wolters!"

"We should talk to Nele," decided Heidi.

"Yes, let's go," Kurt agreed wholeheartedly.

NELE WAS SO ABSORBED IN HER VENGEFUL THOUGHTS that she was startled when she heard a call from behind her.

"Nele, wait a second!"

The Sieverstens. She breathed a sigh of relief; she had assumed it was her boss.

"Moin, Frau Sieversten!" She smiled automatically, something she had learned on the job. Never show your feelings when it comes to the guests, she had been taught. After all, the guest is king.

"Nele... I... both of us," she pointed to her husband, "would like to talk to you in private, somewhere where we won't be disturbed. Would that be possible?"

"What is this about?" Nele wanted to know.

"Can't we discuss this somewhere undisturbed?" Kurt Siversten looked around worriedly, and Nele had the feeling that whatever it was might be something important.

"All right. Come on."

"Coffee, tea?" she asked as the couple sat down on the armchairs offered to them. When they declined, she took a seat.

"Well, what's so important?"

Heidi immediately got to the heart of her request. "It's about

Wolters."

Nele winced. "What about him?"

The couple glanced at each other briefly, and Kurt said firmly, "Like you, we want revenge."

What a strange situation! She swallowed several times and, with difficulty, managed a hoarse, "I beg your pardon?"

The Sieverstens explained that they had overheard her talking to Jan-Ole.

Next, they told her about the death of their daughter and how they had accidentally stumbled across the culprit.

Nele was moved by the story, and she couldn't help tearing up when she thought about what Wolters had done to these people. And then it bubbled out of her.

Wolters had not always been a creep. He could be very nice, and had known what women liked. Even though he didn't look like the typical ladies' man, he had a charismatic personality and could exude charm. Many women liked that. In a weak moment—she had just broken up with a boyfriend—she had succumbed to his wooing. Just for one night!

Later, she said, she'd realized his true character when she'd told him she was pregnant. He had grown angry and yelled at her that she had done this on purpose. He would never acknowledge his paternity. Not at his age! They had then parted ways as best they could on the small Nordic island.

That had been a month ago, when a doctor had confirmed her pregnancy. She was torn about whether to have an abortion or not. On the one hand she wanted to have the baby, but on the other hand she was afraid. Without financial support from Wolters, the future did not look rosy for her. Often enough she had heard of women in similar situations whose lives had not infrequently ended in suicide. She was devastated. She had wanted to meet him today and take her revenge, because he had destroyed her life.

"And how did you imagine this revenge?" asked Heidi.

"Poison," said Nele. "I got myself some poison."

WHEN THE OFFICERS ENTERED THE ROOM, THEY could not believe their eyes.

"Did we get the wrong room?" Thore asked.

"Absolutely not." Kolle was sure this had to be the right room. The electronic door opener can only open a door for which it is programmed.

Wolters had been a bachelor, and in such a man's living quarters, everyone expected a certain degree of untidiness. Kolle knew from his own experience what it could look like in a man's household. Dirty laundry on the armchairs and used towels in the bathroom; empty beer cans on the shelf; all these would have been normal. At least a proper bachelor pad should have dirty dishes from the previous day.

But Wolters didn't seem to fit the stereotype in this regard. Worse, the apartment was the model example of that of a pedant. Clinically clean, Kollerup thought, would fit the bill. The floor was immaculately polished, and the kitchen counter seemed to have been newly installed only yesterday. Even in the cozy sitting area, everything lay as if Wolters had used a ruler and level to precisely align magazines, pictures and cushions. Even the square glass table was exactly in the middle, between the couch and the two armchairs. The books on the single shelf were sorted by size and the color of the cover. A modern version of a sample house from the magazine *Good Housekeeping*.

It was obvious that his colleagues were going to hate searching for evidence here, because it was never easy to find anything usable in an apartment that had been cleaned this way. But Thore believed that a person could only grow when faced with the challenges of life. So they set to work.

Kolle pulled open one drawer after another in a dresser. As expected, carefully folded laundry. In the closet next to it, there were shirts, jackets and pants on hangers. The bathroom was a masterpiece, comparable to any porcelain department in the hardware store. Even the folded towels on the laundry shelf were sorted by color. Kolle didn't have to think long about it. The chief inspector knew very well that Wolters had had a problem.

A call from the living room lured him back. Onne, in overalls that made him seem even smaller, stood in front of the multimedia wall with a bottle in his raised hand. It was an empty bottle of vodka of a brand that could not be bought for less than thirty euros. Kolle looked at him in chastisement. His assistant didn't know any better, so he forgave him for having moved the bottle from the place where he'd found it. Thore carefully placed the bottle on the coffee table and worked it with a powder, then he took a magnifying glass and examined the bottle. "Nothing," he sighed. After that, protected in a ziplock bag, it went into the box for secured material.

Kolle took on the desk—a fragile-looking piece of furniture. Very modern, made of chrome-plated steel elements and a thick glass top. A telephone like a notebook was all that was on the table. No notepad; even the desk pad was spotless. He opened each drawer of the rolling container on the floor. In the lowest one he found stationery with the hotel logo. Nothing odd about that, he said to himself.

Kolle flipped open the notebook, then waited until a technician checked it for fingerprints. In the meantime, he looked at the phone calls the dead man had received. The answering machine was as virginal as a newly installed system. The list of the most recent calls received contained a single number. He pulled out his phone and called Larsson at Husum headquarters.

"Moin, boss," he answered after the second ring.

"Say, Larsson, the dead man's phone—has it been examined yet?"

"Yeah."

"And?"

"Nothing was saved except for the last number dialed, which belonged to Franziska Koch."

"Thank you." Kolle hung up without saying goodbye.

The group moved on to the kitchen. In the refrigerator were ten bottles of the same vodka that Onne had found in the living area, while the dishwasher contained three clean glasses. Nevertheless, they were examined for fingerprints. They found something on one of them—thumb and index fingerprints. Thore immediately said they were so small that they could have come from either a woman or a child. The glass was also bagged.

Then Kolle walked over to the laptop, having been informed by the forensics crew that the device had already been cleaned and checked. He flipped up the screen and switched the computer on. Tidied up as well, of course. But in this case Kolle was grateful, because he could find everything relevant to the case very quickly.

When asked if he could keep it, Thore waved it off. "Sure, if it helps to find the truth."

He was convinced he had seen enough to form a picture of the dead man. With a wave, he indicated to Onne they were leaving.

"Briefing time, Onne. Thore, please call me if you find something important like a confession or something."

They went to the hotel together, into their improvised office, and ordered two liters of coffee and cookies. That had been

Onne's idea. "I would kill for cookies," had been his comment.

"Well," Kolle had said, "if it helps find the truth, please go ahead. But in that case, I'd like to have some of those waffle cookies," he'd specified.

Once they'd received the life-supporting items they wanted, Kolle set to work instantly.

"That beautiful white wall there is our evidence board," he pointed to the wall at the head of the bed, which, like all the beds in the rooms, was a double.

He picked up a felt-tip pen and scrambled onto the bed, almost tripping. Such a beautiful white wall! Then, with a shrug, he wrote the dead man's name in the middle of the wall.

This was nothing special for Onne, who had been known to scribble spontaneous sketches on the wall in his house in Schobüll. So he watched with interest as his Husum artistic kindred spirit embellished the wall.

With pen in hand, Kollerup brought order to their collective thoughts.

"The dead man had ties to the Sieverstens and Christa Hansen. In addition, as we know from Maybach himself, he was in contact with him." He wrote these names in a group on the right side of the wall.

"Wolters arrived on the hallig around four o'clock." He drew a circle around the name of the dead man, then he divided the circle into twelve sections by marking twelve points along the circumference.

"It's a clock!" declared Onne.

Around the four o'clock mark, Kolle drew a line diagonally downward and labeled it "Arrival on the hallig."

From the center left midpoint, at nine o'clock, he drew another line. "Wolters died at exactly nine o'clock in the evening." He marked this line with the word "death."

"The task is to figure out what he did between four in the afternoon and nine in the evening. Where was he, and who was with him?"

"He was probably poisoned during this time period," Onne stated, before adding: "We need to know where Heidi Sierversten, Christa Hansen and Frank Maybach were during that time."

Kolle was proud of his assistant.

"Exactly."

Onne was unstoppable as he continued, "Who had the opportunity, a motive and, of course, the weapon? In our case, the poison."

Kolle was momentarily speechless.

"Alright, we will take these three first." Kollerup circled the names one by one before glancing at the bedside clock.

"After lunch."

"What motive would someone have to poison Wolters?" Onne asked.

"Well, quite simple." Kolle raised his hands and started to count on his fingers. "Poison is almost always a woman's weapon. You don't need strength to use it, nor do you have to make direct contact with a physically superior opponent. Poison is a gentle killer. A knife attack can be warded off. A blow with an object requires force. A firearm is difficult to obtain, makes a hell of a racket, and the recoil, if an untrained person is incapable of holding the gun directly to the victim's head, could result in missed shots. All this requires a certain amount of force because the victim would fight back." Kolle was now holding up ten fingers.

"But poison can be used by men too!" Onne objected.

"Sure," Kollerup confirmed. He concentrated again as he continued. "But I wasn't finished yet. If the poison was administered by a woman, the motive would be a typically female one."

"Now, now," Onne wiggled his index finger punishingly. "You should be careful saying things like that. Men often have 'typical female' motives, I can imagine. And what is a typical female motive? Don't women often... here I'm thinking of my ex-wife... have greed or revenge as a motive?"

Kolle raised his hand in a placating manner as he said, "I was thinking more of jealousy, or even revenge because of rejection. Then there are the women whose husbands have cheated. But I agree greed could also be a motive in our case."

"We can exclude a crime of passion here." That was a very good point, in Kolle's opinion. Amazingly, his assistant was quickly developing into a decent investigator.

"True. Whoever procures poison in order to kill someone with it, or to at least set death in motion, isn't acting in the heat of the moment."

He looked at the wall and added a question mark behind the engineer's name.

"I still don't think poison tends to be a man's weapon of choice," he justified himself. "We'll interrogate Heidi and Kurt first. Because," he enumerated, "they had the opportunity. Their possible motive, revenge, seems the most likely at the moment. The only question is why murder Wolters? Was he the driver who hit their daughter?"

"It's possible," mused Onne.

"Yes, possible. But why would the Sieverstens only now decide to kill Wolters, if..." Kolle raised his voice, "...Wolters was behind the wheel of that car."

"I understand. Too many open questions. Was there nothing in the documents about this?"

Kolle shook his head. "No."

"And the other dossiers on the suspects. What do they say?" asked Onne.

"The only one who would come into question, apart from these three, is Franziska," answered the inspector before asking his assistant to hand him the documents. He leafed through them until he found the relevant passage.

"Aha, here: Koch works part-time as a state-certified mudflat guide."

"Then Koch would have had a motive too!" Onne interjected.

"Which one?" Kolle asked. "Because the silt on Wolters' route is more precious than the silt on hers?"

"No, because there are certain routes in the Wadden Sea that the mudflat guides have to register. Once they do that, that person is the only one allowed to use that route." Onne was surprised that the inspector didn't know this important detail as a coastal resident.

"That would mean," Kolle had closed his eyes to concentrate, "that Wolters might have been removed as a rival."

"Possibly. There's something else you should know. The routes that lead to particularly attractive destinations become more popular over time. That means that those guides earn more money, because more tourists want to tour them."

"Did Wolters have a popular route?"

Onne raised his hands regretfully. "No idea. I only know that such routes usually get passed down to heirs when the owner of the route dies. That's sometimes the only chance other mudflat guides have of acquiring them."

Kollerup wrote Franziska's name on the left side of the wall diagram.

"You shouldn't forget the employees and the two Budniks," Onne reminded him.

"Yes, exactly. We still need to interrogate them."

The names of those just mentioned were written at the bottom of the wall. Svenja, Arne, the cook, Thorsten, his assistant, Maik, the bartender, and Jan-Ole, the technician. Quite a few, Kolle thought.

"Let's focus on these three first," he decided. "The others on our list had contact with Wolters, but he had been the mudflat leader here for many years. What reason would these people have to murder him now?"

"Maybe something happened. I don't know..." Onne let the sentence hang in the air.

Kolle pointed to the wall. "That doesn't change anything. These three first." He tapped the names of the three main suspects. "After we eat."

At that moment the door flew open. Of course it was Bernd, the hotel manager. Before he could make a sound, Kolle said from his position on the bed, "Let me guess! Something's happened, or someone really wants to talk to me on the phone!"

"It's your colleagues from the forensics department. They're finished."

"Can't they call on the phone?"

"No, they're down in the fitness... uh, provisional headquarters now."

"We're coming!"

When the two investigators arrived in the gym, their jaws dropped. Labeled plastic boxes were piled up against the walls, and items were scattered across the tables. The crime scene investigators were bustling about, talking on phones, and frantically tapping away on their laptops. Questions buzzed around the room, and answers were hollered back.

The head of the crime scene investigators wordlessly handed Kollerup a cup of coffee and indicated he wanted to show him something. There were file folders on a table. Their spines were labeled with a combination of letters and numbers, but that wasn't what he wanted to show Kolle. On the open laptop monitor, the one belonging to the dead man, he caught sight of photos, very intimate photos. It was easy enough to recognize the young lady who had served him breakfast on the terrace. It was Nele!

HALLIG
The day of the storm
6 p.m.

NELE WAS DETERMINED TO GET HER REVENGE!

After the conversation with the Sieverstens, she was absolutely sure she was doing the right thing. They had given her the poison they had procured, looking ridiculously banal as it did in its plastic cup. She opened the vodka bottle and refined her poison cocktail with Heidi's ingredient. Then she carefully closed the bottle and called Jan-Ole. "I am leaving now," she said and hung up.

On her way to Wolters' apartment, which had a separate entrance, she ran into Maybach, who was walking back toward the hotel. Without greeting her, he hurried past as if he hadn't noticed her. Nele wondered what a hotel guest was doing talking to the mudflat guide at this hour.

When Kai opened the door, he grinned sullenly.

"Well, come on in. Take off your shoes."

As if in a defensive reaction, she held the bottle in front of his stomach and murmured, "Here. I brought this with me. Maybe we can calmly talk things over."

Without taking his eyes off her, he accepted the bottle.

"Sit down!" The apartment was, as always, clinically clean. Kai went to the kitchen and fetched two glasses.

"You're joining me, aren't you?" he called affably into the living room, ever the jovial host.

"Oh, that's alright...I won't. The baby," she called back

apologetically, like a guest who refuses a drink because she is indisposed at the moment. "But you're welcome to bring me some water."

"Water?" He seemed to have lost some of his gracious spirit. She heard the water rushing as he filled the glasses.

"So, tell me how you've been," he remarked innocently. As if they were still the best of friends! She couldn't breathe for a moment.

"You know..."

He interrupted her. "What do I know?"

"Well, the baby."

"What baby? You're pregnant! Who's the lucky father?"

She couldn't believe her ears. Hadn't they recently quarreled, and hadn't he threatened her? Didn't she say he had obligations as the father? It seemed like a dream to her. He took a sip and clicked his tongue with relish.

"Good vodka. The only one to have! Too bad you're missing it."

He took another deep sip and refilled his glass, which this time was filled to the rim.

She took a quick sip of her water and toasted him.

"But, getting back to your alleged pregnancy... I think you should have an abortion. Think about it. You're still young, and a child will screw up your life."

"No, Kai. I want to keep it."

He took a thoughtful sip and put the glass down before leaning toward Nele. "We've been through this," he whispered with a grim expression. And then he actually patted her cheek.

She endured this with her mouth agape. As if nothing had happened, he sat up straight again and drank a big gulp. Then he poured himself another drink.

"You know," he began softly, "I haven't had it easy lately. Just today, my tour was cancelled. I know damn well that Budnik is up to something!"

For a moment, he gazed motionless out the window. Suddenly he shouted, "And here you come with your claim to be having my child!" Shaking his head, he stood up and instantly toppled back onto his chair like a wet sack.

"Whaa havvv ...you puut in thee vodka?" he slurred with crossed eyes as he passed out.

After Nele had cleaned up any traces of her presence, she couldn't resist and punched the unconscious man in the face. There, that's what you get! she thought bitterly. Then she called Jan-Ole. "It's time!"

Nobody noticed Jan-Ole and Nele as they stowed Wolters, well-packed in a carpet, in the vehicle. The guests were in the hotel getting ready for dinner, and the other staff members were working. The artist-shepherd was busy at the old church bringing his sheep to safety. Anyone who might have seen them would have thought they were just two employees going about their work. They drove to the jetty and deposited the unconscious man at the edge of the mudflat. They told themselves that when the tide came in that night, it would do the rest. Besides, the storm was looming as a threatening black wall in the west. As the sun was swallowed up by the storm front, the temperature dropped noticeably, and gusts of wind announced the change in the weather. With that, they drove back to the loading bay at the hotel.

The first raindrops began to fall as Nele and Jan-Ole went back to work.

HOTEL
Second day after the storm
12:30 p.m.

KOLLE WASN'T SURE IF HE COULD STILL unselfconsciously look Nele in the eyes; the photos had been burned into his brain.

Onne took it all in stride. In his opinion, Nele had always been impressive, and even though he was now acquainted with details of her body that hardly anyone got to see, he didn't think it was worth mentioning.

They were sitting in the restaurant area, since the terrace wasn't open yet. The outdoor bar no longer existed and was presumably drifting somewhere out on the North Sea. Tables and chairs were piled up in disorderly heaps, ready to be hauled off as trash. Someone had opened the door to let in some fresh air. Outside the sun was shining, as if it wanted to make the destruction on the hallig look nicer. If you closed your eyes, you could almost think that everything was normal: a beautiful summer day in the Wadden Sea. But the chaos left by the storm marred this impression. It would probably take days to repair the worst of the damage.

They ate in a silence that was only occasionally punctuated by a "Salt, please," or "Pass the pepper."

Kolle wasn't aware of what he was eating, and once his appetite was abated, he pushed his plate to the side. Of all people, Nele, he thought in despair.

He felt as old as the hills when he rose to notify the guests that he was ready.

Without a preliminary explanation, he said, "Kurt and Heidi, I would like you to meet me at 2 p.m. in my provisional office. This will not be a casual conversation, so please consider this a formal summons to an interrogation. I've already discussed with you several times the unusual circumstances surrounding Wolters' death."

He glanced uncertainly at the counter in the kitchen, behind which the kitchen crew was gathered.

"Nele, please make yourself available to talk with me at three o'clock. Then, after a short break, I'd like to see Frank and Marianne at half past four. Christa, your turn will be at half past six. Tomorrow morning, after breakfast at ten, Franziska and Ilona. Any questions?"

Kollerup took a deep breath and longed for a sip of beer. Since no one seemed to have any questions, he waved at Onne to follow him.

They walked into the gym, where Cartensen was already waiting for them. Now that the rest of the team was on break, they were the only ones in the room. Thore led them to a table which was covered with the files Kolle had already seen.

"Wolters left behind some rather revealing notes. Thank God he was a compulsive neatnik." He gestured at the folder. "Wolters was in contact with Christa Hansen, Frank Maybach and Franziska Koch. He didn't have a direct personal relationship with Koch, but he did have a significant tie to her as a mudflat guide. Apparently Franziska was new to the mudflat tour business. Then there is the connection to Hansen and the Maybachs through the wind turbines."

"It isn't news to me that the three of them are, or were, active in the same industry. None of this applies to Wolters any more."

"That was the most important thing I had to tell you at the moment. We've now examined practically the entire hallig, except for the pile of garbage at the jetty. There won't be any usable clues there."

"Have you checked the guests' rooms too?"

"Yep. There was something in Koch's room that might interest you."

Thore pointed at a plastic container, and the officers took a look at the contents together. A small brown glass bottle with a measurement dropper in the lid.

"What's this?" Kolle held the bag up to the light. In the bottle sloshed a liquid.

"According to Ms. Koch, a homeopathic remedy."

"And?"

"With the rapid tests we have at our disposal, it wasn't what paralyzed Wolters."

"So not ricin or that drug in the poison cocktail, the one Lührssen identified?"

"No, sir. But..." Kolle lurked. There was always a concluding punchline whenever Thore announced his findings. Must be some kind of disease, like Lührssen exhibited, whenever he exclaims "Guess what?" Kolle thought.

"But," Thore continued, "it is E605."

"Oh, God!" exclaimed Kolle. "How old school is that?"

Thore threw his arms in the air and chirruped, "There you go!"

WOLTERS BEGAN TO STIR IN THE RISING WATER. OH, the pain! His stomach was burning like hell. Then he realized where he was lying, while rain poured into his open mouth. He coughed and spat. With difficulty and groaning, he managed to turn onto his stomach. Gasping, he braced himself with his arms on the stony embankment. Ah! He felt infinitely tired, but a remnant of sense told him that he had better not wait a moment longer to try to get ashore. If only the burning would stop! Propped up on his forearms, the contents of his stomach reappeared. He had to get out of here now, an inner voice urged.

What time is it? Never mind. Just get out of here. His senses were gradually returning. He could now hear the rush of the rain and the howling of the storm. He felt the slight pain as the storm hurled raindrops across his face. He tasted blood in his mouth.

After the first flash of lightning, his memory came back. Nele, the vodka and the nebulous shreds of the memory of a short, bumpy ride in a vehicle. He also saw another face, Jan-Ole! Then nothing else.

He finally reached the paved road to the hotel. It was pitch dark; where he had always previously seen lights at night, across on the other islands, there was nothing except blackness. Only the outside lights of the haubarg were burning. Good. That's where I have to go, he thought grimly. He needed to tell the others about Nele, who had tried to poison him! That bitch! A dizzy spell made him collapse again. He turned over on his back and breathed in water again and gasped. Come on! You have to get up! He struggled back onto his stomach and pushed himself up again. Then he stood up, shivering, in the storm. Where was the light? It was gone! Only a blackness that looked absolute. He blinked. Streaks of light appeared before his eyes. What the hell was going on?

"You must keep going!" shouted a voice. Who was it? Had someone shouted? Had he just imagined it? No matter, go on. He lost his bearings, stumbled over some grass, and fell over a section of fence.

An infinitely long time passed, then the smell of the sheep! He hated sheep, but now he was cheering inside. The church! There was a light on inside the church, not much or even bright, but it was like the star of Bethlehem. Panting and with a grin on his face, he collapsed in front of the entrance. Here he was protected from the storm. He sat on the sandy path in the pouring rain and vomited. His mouth tasted like iron, and he tried to spit it out. The vomiting fit felt like it lasted an eternity.

When he had recovered somewhat, he pulled himself together. To the hotel! It wasn't far! The storm was now getting more turbulent. From far away, light once again glittered across his retina. Now he knew where he was. Behind the hotel. The terrace. Not far! Go, go! Swaying, with the storm at his back, his going was no easier than before. He had to be careful that the gusts didn't throw him to the ground. He stumbled when something hit him in the back. The pain made him cry out again.

The hurricane was howling in his ears now, drowning out all the other sounds as if it were a single wind ensemble. He was the storm! He had started to howl along with it when a piece of corrugated iron came flying through the air and brushed against him. Across his neck. Warm liquid warmed his neck and his upper body. That was good! His strength came back, propelling him forward along with the storm. He tripped over an object and fell far. He fell oh so slowly, and for what felt like forever. In slow motion, objects flew past him in the light streaming from the bar, as if against a black screen. He hardly felt himself touching the ground. So close to his goal! No, he couldn't give up! The warming stream from his neck slowly dried up. Remnants of it mixed with the rain that was washing him clean. He shook his head to rid himself of a fatigue unlike any he had ever felt before. Whew! He shouldn't have done that! Dizziness gripped him, and his heart raced. Onward!

Now he was standing in front of the dwelling mound and swaying in the storm. He dropped onto his arms and dragged himself up the six meters to the terrace. He recognized the people who were reveling in the storm. Yes! Look, I'm coming! He leaned on one of the windows. Why won't you open? He gazed into Christa's face as a deep sadness overcame him. Too late! A lightning bolt hissed into the water nearby as the lights went out. He missed out on the subsequent second lightning strike.

In the lashing rain and roaring hurricane Kai Wolters took his last breath.

HOTEL
Second day after the storm
2:00 p.m.

HEIDI AND KURT SAT AT THE TABLE WITH THEIR heads hanging down. Onne switched on the tablet so that he could easily start the recording when needed. Behind him was the camera, also ready.

Kolle hadn't been idle since their meal, but had been reading through the dossiers of all those involved. He was prepared.

"How are the two of you doing today? Would you like something to drink? Coffee or tea?" he began the interrogation.

"I'd like some tea," Heidi said shyly. Kurt was satisfied without having a drink, so Onne jumped up to get what Heidi had requested.

"That storm the day before yesterday was bad, wasn't it?" Kolle made small talk to thaw the ice that had built up since the day before.

Heidi sighed, and Kurt wobbled his head uncertainly.

"Must be climate change," he grumbled.

"Is that what you think, Kurt?" Kolle prodded.

"Yes, you read about it all the time."

"Maybe so. I don't get to read much myself. The job, you know how it is. A lot of work and hardly any time."

"Yes. When we were running our business, we didn't have much free time either."

"Well, then I'm sure you understand how I feel." Kolle pretended to be a man at the end of his tether, whose professional plate was packed to overflowing. "Oh well, back to the grind," he patted a file cover a couple of times. It looked like a real file.

"This case! I'm getting desperate." He shook his head like a detective on the verge of giving up. "It seems to have been murder, as you know."

Heidi's nose turned a little paler than usual.

"Yes, we know."

Onne came in with some tea, sugar and milk, before sitting down and starting the equipment.

"Yes, as I said... this case." Kolle turned the first blank page of the file, which he held at an angle in front of him. His eyes wandered over the sheet as if he were reading.

"What did you think of Wolters, as a person?"

They both glanced at each other. Heidi shrugged, and Kurt pursed his mouth.

"The same that you'd think of any other mudflat guide," Heidi tried to explain.

"We didn't meet him until we got here," Kurt added, to assist his wife.

She looked at him and added, "Well... how should I put it... he was probably a nice person. Always friendly and polite, joking with the guests and stuff."

"Exactly. And the things he knew!" recalled Kurt.

"Yes, as a mudflat guide you have to know a lot of things!" Heidi agreed.

Kolle replied with a smile, "Yes, exactly! He was a local, after all! Wait—" he pretended to read the file. "Ah, yes. Here," he tapped the sheet. "He originally came from Föhr. That's funny."

"What's funny?" Kurt demanded.

"Well! You're from Föhr too!"

Silence.

Heidi's teacup wobbled slightly in her hand, which hesitated halfway to her mouth.

"So what?" Kurt tried to play the hardened one. "Do you know everyone from Husum, Kolle?"

"No, of course not!" Kollerup answered dismissively with a grin. Aha, he thought, he answered a question I didn't even ask. "But Theo Knudsen from Wyk, you must know him!" he declared jovially, like someone trying to help out a friend. That was Heidi Sievertsen's uncle, through whom Wolters was related to them. He sent a silent thank you to Larsson, who had researched this detail.

Heidi now put down her tea, having probably lost her thirst.

"What about him?" she asked in a shaky voice.

"Well, that's your uncle, Heidi! That's what it says here." Kollerup tapped the blank page in front of him.

"Could be." Kurt drew his eyebrows together and scowled at Kolle.

"And he used to be married to Sinje Hansen." Kolle studied the couple perplexedly, as if they were being strangely obtuse. "But that's not really all that important. What's more significant is that Wolters was Sinje's nephew!"

"We don't know any Wolters from Alkersum!" exclaimed Kurt.

"Oh, I see. It was just a thought, seeing as your daughter was, at that time, a student at the Eilun Feer Skuul, the high school in Wyk. Just like Wolters had been." That hit home. Their eyes widened.

"But you can't know everyone on Föhr." Kolle spread his hands apologetically. He hadn't known that the dead man had come from Alkersum, but that didn't matter. He had gotten what he'd wanted.

"I'll ask you again. Did you know Wolters before you came to stay here on the hallig?"

Heidi and Kurt visibly slumped.

"Yes." Heidi stared at Kolle defiantly.

"Did Wolters have your daughter on his conscience?"

"There's no point in denying it anymore. Yes, Wolters hit and killed our daughter." As Heidi told the story of how they had learned of Wolters' guilt, Kurt took hold of his wife's left hand and squeezed it.

"And you were going to confront him here?"

"Heidi, it's no use lying," Kurt whispered.

"We didn't kill him!" his wife cried desperately.

"We'll continue this tomorrow. You may go now."

Kolle signaled to Onne, who stood up and switched the equipment to stand-by.

"I should actually place you under temporary arrest, but since we're living in a prison here as it is, I don't think you'll be leaving the hallig. Otherwise I'd have to issue a warrant for your arrest. You know what that would mean, don't you?"

"Yes, Kolle." Two thin-mouthed Sievertsens crept out of the room.

He carefully bagged the cup from which Heidi had drunk her tea, labeled it, and told Onne to give it to the forensics team.

HOTEL
Second day after the storm
3:00 p.m.

NELE PETERSEN, TO CALL HER BY HER FULL NAME, SAT bolt upright and gazed intently at the Husum detective.

Kolle was once again holding a placebo file cover, as he called it, but it was now enriched with spicy photos. His embarrassment had subsided. "You have to be professional about it," was his answer to Onne's question about how he was dealing with it.

The equipment was up and running, and they had gone through the usual introductory procedure.

"Do you know the dead man?"

"Yes. Kai is our tidal flat guide. Uh, was our former guide. He's dead now." This seemed to tickle her for some reason; a few laugh lines had formed around her eyes.

"We know you're from Amrum," he declared as he thumped the file cover. "Isn't it possible that you might have met him at some point in the past?"

"You mean before he offered his guided tours out here? No, I hadn't." Quite controlled and attentive.

"Well, all right. You might have. Amrum and Föhr aren't all that far apart." He groaned dramatically and gazed at her pleadingly. "It isn't an easy case! Is there anything you can tell us that would be helpful?"

"I'd love to. But how?"

"You know everyone here on the hallig. Just between us. Who do you think could commit murder?"

"No one, actually."

"Yeah, right. Stupid question." Kolle seemed abashed, but he didn't give up. "Wasn't there some fight between the guests or the staff and Wolters?"

"Oh, I don't know about that. I do my work and keep my nose out of other people's business. I like my job."

"You've been working here for so long. Did Wolters ever hint in conversation or make some remark that someone was mad at him?"

"Let me think." She gazed pensively out the window with thoughtful, narrowed eyes. "Yes. He had a fight with Budnik once. Budnik had wanted to revise his route, because there was another guide who was taking a different route."

"Oh, yeah? Tell me about it."

"That would be Mommsen. He goes out to the seal sandbar, and Budnik thinks that's more interesting, even if you're not allowed to actually go out onto the sandbank. But you can see them well without disturbing the animals. Wolters got really bent out of shape about that."

"So, Budnik. Interesting." Kolle tapped nervously on the file. "Nothing else?"

"No, not really."

"Well, then." Kolle flipped open the file. "You may go. That's all," he muttered, without looking up. As Nele stood up, smiling, and was about to turn away, her eyes fell on the photos. Kollerup had spun them around so that she had to see them.

Nele cupped her hands in front of her mouth and gasped loudly, her eyes huge.

"Maybe you should sit down again." Kolle fanned them out on the table. Nele's features twisted into a grimace.

"That pig!" she screamed, ripping the page of photos in a burst of rage. Kolle turned over a new page in the file. The same pictures.

"You can tear them up all you like, Nele." With that, he flipped over more pages. The file was full of the snapshots. "Now please tell me what you did to Wolters."

"I didn't do anything! Anything! What do you think I did? I have nothing to blame myself for!" she sobbed.

"How long were you together?"

"A year."

"And?"

"At first, I thought he was boring. But he could be so likeable, so charming and sensitive too." She was crying fiercely now.

"And then?"

"Then what? I don't understand."

"What happened after a year?"

"I found out he just wanted to get me in bed, that's what happened!"

"So he was just using you, you mean?"

"Yes! These," she pointed at the tattered photographs, "he took them secretly. I didn't know about it."

"Did you know about these pictures before now?"

"Yes, I came across them by accident on his computer. When he was asleep one night, I started up his laptop, just to look something up online."

"Then you found the pictures."

"Yes, that was when everything ended." She had regained her composure and seemed calmer.

"Did you confront him about the pictures?"

"Yes. He just laughed. I shouldn't act like that, he said."

"When was that?"

"Last February."

"You haven't been in contact with him since then?"

"No. We've been avoiding each other."

"Do you know what ricin is?"

"No. What is it?" The answer was an honest one, Kollerup realized. He considered this development. Could the secretly-taken pictures be a motive? Possibly. People had been killed for much less.

"Where were you on the day of the storm, between 4 and 9 p.m.?"

"I had the afternoon off. My shift started at eight o'clock, since I was on the night shift."

"What did you do that afternoon?"

"I took a nap after lunch. I got up around five, and after that, I watched a little TV and then went out for a short walk."

"Did anyone see you?"

"Yes, the Sievertsens."

"Good, Nele. That's all for now. You may go, but please stay close by today. I might have some more questions later."

"This is getting more and more interesting!" Onne obviously found it all incredibly exciting.

"So, what have we got?" Kolle was trying to get his thoughts in order. He stood up and wandered around the room.

"First, there are the Sievertsens, whose daughter was killed by an unknown assailant decades ago. They finally learned who killed their daughter. Then there's Nele, an exploited and humiliated woman. Who had the most serious reason to kill Wolters?"

"If it were me, and my daughter got murdered, and I saw the perpetrator get away scot-free, I know what I'd do." For Onne, the matter was clear.

Kolle agreed with him on that point.

"It's understandable that the parents would want to avenge their child. But what about a humiliated woman?" Kolle gazed at Onne, perplexed.

"Yes, true. Plus, she had time enough to prepare everything," Onne added.

"We'll have to question the Sievertsens again tomorrow, that's for sure."

Just as they were about to leave the room—it had been ages since Kolle's last cigarette—they collided with Budnik.

"Guess what just happened!" he shouted.

Kolle had had enough of these stupid games. "Spit it out!"

"Jan-Ole has abducted Nele! He's barricaded the two of them in the generator shed, and is threatening to murder her!"

HALLIG
Second day after the storm
3:30 p.m.

JAN-OLE WAS NERVOUS. OVER AND OVER AGAIN, HE told himself that he had done the right thing. He had to help his Nele! This delicate creature, so innocent and so exploited! He couldn't stand to see her suffering, which was why he had suggested to her that she help him get rid of Wolters. He had decided long ago, anyway, that no one would be allowed to harm his Nele! Back in the spring, when he had noticed that she seemed constantly sad, he began to win her over to his idea, and his plan took shape. They would get their revenge on Wolters! And so he procured everything he would need to carry out his plot.

It had been easy enough to administer the ricin to Wolters. One beer and then another, every day a little bit in his drinks. When Wolters complained of heartburn, Jan-Ole gave him a remedy for it. "An old home remedy, guaranteed to work," he had assured Wolters. And then two days before the storm, a godsend landed in Jan-Ole's lap when he'd found several ancient beer bottles in the mudflats during a hike. He'd filled them with ricin and beer, before sealing them with wax. Everyone would think they were old bottles that had been waiting to be discovered for the past century. Wolters and he had opened one of them just for fun and tasted the beer. Of course, he'd only pretended to sample it, so that

Wolters wouldn't suspect anything. Wolters had exclaimed in amazement that the beer tasted excellent, considering how old the stuff was.

When he saw her after the interrogation, he knew that something had happened. She needed him! He intercepted her on the way to the staff lodge.

"Nele! What's wrong?" he asked her. She sobbed with abandon on his shoulder, and they sat down on one of the benches that stood beside the path.

"It's over! The police know everything!"

"Know what?" He gazed deeply into her red-rimmed eyes.

"Oh, the guy from the police found out that I was with Wolters! And he's going to find out about the pregnancy soon too!"

"Nele! Nele, listen to me!" He shook her by the shoulders. "No one will know."

"There's no point anymore."

"Nele! You and I have a future together! I will take care of you!"

"You?" Nele looked at him in amazement.

"Yes. Me!"

"What did you do to Wolters?"

"Nothing he didn't deserve."

"Did you kill him?"

"Me? You were the one who wanted revenge! I only helped!"

"But I didn't want to kill him! Teach him a lesson, yes, but not kill him!"

"Really? I remember everything quite differently! What about the Sievertsens? Didn't they also give you their poison so that Wolters would definitely die?"

"Yes, but that was a sleeping pill! Wolters was supposed to be only—"

"Only what?" he interrupted her. Jan-Ole couldn't believe it! He had been so nice and helpful to his beloved, and this was the thanks he got?

"You were going to kill him! Why would someone do

something like that? Knock him out and dump him at the water's edge? And then everything was going to be good again?" He stood up and positioned himself in front of her. "Oh, sorry, my mistake! It won't happen again?" he mimicked Wolters' voice. He grabbed her and shouted at her. "Wake up! I'm your protector!"

"You? Get lost! I'm going to tell the inspector everything!"

"You're not going to do that!"

He dragged her on her feet, then he punched her. She hung limply in his arms as he hurried to the generator shed.

Malte Maybach, who was watching, immediately ran to the hotel and alerted Budnik.

GENERATOR SHED
Second day after the storm
4:15 p.m.

"JAN-OLE! OPEN UP! WHAT'S GOING ON?" KOLLE WAS standing in front of the steel door, the only entrance to the generator shed. There were windows on one side of the building, but they were too high to see what was going on inside.

From inside, Jan-Ole's voice boomed indistinctly, "Get out of here, or I'll kill her!"

Kolle turned to Budnik, who was standing behind him. "Is there a telephone inside? Or do you have Jan-Ole's cell number?"

"Something better. I have a radio, and he has one in his pocket too. It's faster than a phone." He handed the detective a device no bigger than a pack of cigarettes.

"Here is the talk button," he pointed to a button on the side. Kolle nodded and said to the guests standing around him, "Please go back into the hotel. You can't do anything anyway."

He pressed the button and said, "Jan-Ole? Can you hear me? Please report."

One short beep and the technician answered, "I want to be taken to the mainland by helicopter. I'll need a vehicle ready and waiting there. Full tank, no tracker."

"All right, but it will take a while," answered Kolle.

"Yeah, sure. That's what you always say."

"Is Nele okay?"

"As well as she can be."

"Is there something you want to tell us? Did you kill Wolters?"

Onne held a small digital dictaphone up to the radio while Kolle spoke to the kidnapper. For a few seconds, there was rustling on the speaker.

"Yes, I killed Wolters. He hurt Nele. My Nele."

"How did you do it?"

"You know that, cop!"

"I want to hear it from you."

"Ricin. I've been giving him ricin for months. Last Friday's dose was supposed to kill him!"

Kolle whispered in response to Onne, "Did you get that?" The latter just nodded.

"Jan-Ole! Listen to me now." He waved Thore towards him.

"The head of forensics is standing next to me. His name is Thore."

"Yes, and?"

"He'll tell you when the helicopter will be available."

"Hey, Jan-Ole. This is Thore."

"Fuck off!"

"We have to send for the helicopter from the mainland first. It'll take an hour at the most."

"Are you fucking kidding me?"

"No. You know what's happening on the mainland."

"Make that forty-five minutes."

In the background, Nele could be heard calling indistinctly, then the connection died.

"Is there another way into the building?" Kolle asked the hotel owner.

"There used to be a door from the gym, but we walled it up."

"What is behind the wall in the shed?"

"The generator."

"Right against the wall?"

"No, just about a meter in front of it."

"Do you have the blueprints for the shed?"

"Yes, I'll get them." He strode off.

"Jan-Ole?"

"What do you want, Kolle?"

"Give me Nele."

"No way. I'll call you back in forty-five minutes." Click and done.

"Onne, you stay here and keep watch." Onne nodded.

Kollerup had to make a phone call now, undisturbed. In his makeshift office, he stood in front of the wall where he had painted his case diagram and thought about what had happened.

The technician had not even been on his radar, but Nele, who'd had an affair with Wolters, had been. Jan-Ole had confessed that he had poisoned Wolters with ricin. That was information only the perpetrator could have had. Kolle had only told the guests that the mudflat guide had most likely been killed with poison, and thus only the perpetrator could have known that ricin had been involved. As it looked, there had to be at least one other attacker of whom Jan-Ole knew nothing. Or didn't want to name, to protect Nele. "My Nele," the technician had said.

But the Sieverstens were the next closest candidates, more likely than Franziska Koch, for example. The Sieverstens—he needed to interrogate them thoroughly again. The other trail, which led to the wind turbine industry, was no longer so hot. He could follow up on that one later.

He pulled out his phone and called Larsson.

"Moin, boss," his colleague in Husum answered.

"Moin, Larsson. New situation. A witness has been taken hostage. I need a helicopter urgently, any one."

"Yes, I know. Thore has already called Eysenhardt."

"Please put a rush on it."

"Sure, boss."

"And Larsson—the helicopter shouldn't be able to leave the hallig once it gets here."

"Fuel problems, boss?"

"We understand each other."

"Always, boss. Anything else?"

"One more thing. Mr. and Mrs. Sieversten, see if one of them suffers from insomnia."

"Is that all?" Larsson sighed and started hammering away on his keyboard.

Kolle, meanwhile, went into the restaurant with his phone to his ear and ordered two large coffees with hand signals. "Regular, not French press!" he whispered. With his cell phone wedged between his ear and his shoulder, he went to the generator shed and handed Onne one of the coffees.

"Boss?" his Husum colleague finally called out. "Bingo. Mr. Sieversten regularly takes a strong prescription sleeping pill. I won't even try to pronounce the name of the drug."

"The same as we found in Wolters?"

"Wait a minute... yes, the same."

"Would you take another look at the final report from Larsson to see if that was the only drug in him besides ricin?"

"Since you're asking me so nicely—hold on."

In the meantime, he turned to his assistant, "Was there anything else, Onne?"

"Nothing. I heard voices once, but nothing specific. Sounded like an argument."

Larsson answered. "Boss, you should've been a professional bingo player."

"So, that means no?"

"No, that's all there was."

"Thank you. I'll think of you later when I say my prayers, Larsson."

"Amen," came his short reply. Both hung up at the same time.

THE END
Second day after the storm
5:30 p.m.

THE AIR WAS THICK IN THE ROOM. ICY SILENCE STRUCK the Sieverstens as they gazed into the detective's face. The equipment was running in the background as Kolle murmured, "Please sit down."

The two knew immediately what was in store for them, so, for Kurt, there was only one way forward.

"We admit everything. Together with Nele, we planned to kill Wolters."

"Why with Nele of all people?"

"Well, because she was pregnant with Wolters' child. Didn't you know that?" He hadn't known that, but he didn't let on.

"Unfortunately, Nele can't say anything about that right now, but I'll ask her as soon as Jan-Ole lets her go."

Kolle had his placebo file with him again. He opened it and said, "Well, tell me about it."

"You already know everything. What else should we say?"

"Everything from the beginning. I have time."

After half an hour, the couple left the room, and silence reigned there again. Kolle pulled out his phone and notified Larsson about the current situation. He promised to take care of the warrants immediately. Since they had recorded everything from both confessors, the rest was just a formality.

"The helicopters are on their way, boss."

"Alright, thanks for thinking of that."

"The first one should actually almost be there. As you requested, it won't be able to leave the hallig. Someone must've forgotten to fill it up before take-off."

Then Kolle did something he should have done a long time ago. He took the confiscated pistol from the safe, put a magazine in the grip, and loaded it.

Back at the generator shed, nothing had changed. Onne was sitting in the shade on a bench, having dozed off.

"No news," his assistant greeted him. Kolle sat down next to Onne. They discussed the case while gazing out over the summery hallig and watching the sheep ruminate. Kolle went through all the facts they had so far about the Sieverstens' complicity and the fact that Nele had been pregnant with Wolters' baby and that he had left her. He also mentioned that Nele still had to be questioned on that point. Had she, like the avenging parents, also contributed a poison to the mix? Kolle pulled out his phone and called Thore.

After a brief greeting, Thore informed him that they were now finished. He would join them in a minute and report the preliminary final result of the forensics.

"Tell me, did you find anything interesting when you searched Nele's room?" Kolle asked. At the same moment, Thore stepped out of the haubarg.

"Yes, we did, guess what...?"

"Thore!"

"Alright, alright. We found the same stuff that knocked Wolters out in Nele's room. An opened pack of the substance, the name of which I don't expect you to know."

"And you also searched Jan-Ole's apartment?"

"Of course. Ricin in an old beer bottle."

Onne suddenly became anxious and fidgety.

"A beer bottle?" he asked uncertainly.

"Yes, it could have come straight from Rungholdt. Why?"

"Oh, shit."

But Kolle already knew what his temporary colleague was getting at. He patted the shoulder of the now obviously shocked man.

"Don't panic. That's not enough for a murder charge."

"Man! That's what I kept wanting to tell you!"

"Wolters gave it to you. I know."

"How did you...?"

"Because you're just not the type to go into the mudflats."

"Why is that?" the pint-sized painter-shepherd turned temporarily-appointed policeman was furious.

"Because you... well," Kolle searched for a diplomatic answer. "Because you're more of a land guy. That's why."

The rumble of the helicopter brought them back to reality. Thore and Kollerup went off to brief the pilot on the situation, right before the radio in Kolle's pocket went off.

"It's about time!"

"Your wish is our command, Jan-Ole."

"All fueled up? And the car is waiting for me over there?"

"Everything as you wish. Do you need a police escort?"

"No, I don't. Let me know when you're ready!"

Kolle told the pilot what to do, instructing him to make a low-level circuit over the hallig, at least as far as the jetty. He had no desire to get his feet wet.

"All clear, Inspector. I know what to do, and if necessary, I can simulate an engine failure. No problem there. Is the perp armed?"

"I don't know, but probably at least with a knife or a hammer."

Back at the generator shed, they hid behind the half-opened

back door of the hotel.

"Jan-Ole, your taxi's ready and waiting."

The door of the generator house opened, and Nele was pushed out, a long knife blade at her neck. Jan-Ole pressed close to her body, the radio in his free hand.

"Get out of here! Otherwise, she'll die!" he shouted with a searching look. "Where are you cop pigs?"

Kolle motioned for the others to remain quiet.

"We're nowhere close," he whispered into his radio. "The helicopter is ready. You can board."

"Is the pilot there too?"

"Of course."

"I'm going now. No tricks!"

He pushed Nele forward. "Go on!" he snarled at her. She seemed unharmed, but was rigid with fear. She stumbled toward the sound of the engine, her captor close against her back. Kolle and his colleagues, counting Onne among them, ran straight through the hotel to the front entrance. All the guests were gathered in the restaurant, seeking shelter in a group. Kolle made a placating gesture and only said, "Won't be long now."

Then they were at the front door. They watched as the man and his captive climbed in under the spinning rotor blades, then the helicopter slowly took off, spun on its axis, and flew slowly at head height toward the jetty. The three policemen sprinted off. There the engine started to spit, stopped once, and then howled briefly. They had reached it by the time the engine had stopped with a plop. Like a stone, the helicopter plummeted to the grass as the rotor came to a halt. The machine bounced twice and tipped precariously to one side. Balancing on one skid, the machine couldn't decide which side to tip toward. The wrong side won out. Kolle pulled out his gun and ran for his life. Actually, he was running for Nele's life.

Arriving at the helicopter, which lay there like a crushed dragonfly, he jumped onto the skid, tore open the door and held the pistol ready to fire into the machine. The pilot was in the process of punching the kidnapper, and Jan-Ole collapsed powerless. Nele seemed unhurt, though unconscious.

With the pilot's help, he pulled Jan-Ole out of the machine and dragged him onto the ground. Two seconds later, he was lying on the ground, tied up with two cable ties.

Thore and Onne tended to Nele. When she opened her eyes, the cavalry was already there. Fortunate, Kolle thought with a grin.

When he saw who all were getting out of the second, huge Bundeswehr helicopter, Kolle wondered who was actually holding down the fort back in Husum. First Eysenhardt, then Lührssen, and finally Larsson. In addition, two officers who instantly flanked Jan-Ole at a wave from Kollerup. Lührssen immediately took in the situation, bent over Nele, and began to examine her.

"Well, Kolle!" droned the prosecutor. "Once again, you've done a great job!" He pointed at the crashed helicopter and patted him on the shoulder. "But, well, the end justifies the means, doesn't it?"

Kolle ignored him and greeted his colleague Larsson, before introducing him to Onne, who grew embarrassed when he was praised in the highest terms. Kollerup thought that those two, Larsson and Onne, could be a good team. The beanpole and the short guy. They obviously took an instant liking to each other.

Eysenhardt was holding four arrest warrants, with which he first arrested the Sieverstens and then Jan-Ole, one after the other, though not without the obligatory reading of their rights.

Then he took Kolle aside. "You can deal with this one better than I could," he muttered sheepishly with a wink.

Kollerup didn't quite know what to do with this arrest warrant. In desperation, he folded it up and stuck it in a trouser pocket.

Nele was lying strapped to a stretcher, covered with a horsehair army blanket. She smiled at him.

"I know. You have to arrest me now," she breathed weakly.

"I know that too. Good luck to both of you," Kollerup replied in a strained voice.

When they put the pregnant woman in the helicopter, Kolle promised with a lump in his throat, "Everything will work itself out."

Following that, those who had to get back to the mainland boarded the helicopter as well. Christa Hansen had urgent appointments on the mainland and was also allowed to leave the hallig.

After the helicopter had made another circle, Eysenhardt saluted those remaining on the island, and then it was quiet once more on the hallig.

"Larsson! You've really dressed up for the island," Kollerup praised his colleague that evening. He was wearing white Bermuda shorts, a colorful, neatly ironed shirt, and immaculate white sneakers on his feet. They sat together with Thore and Onne in the circle of guests who had decided to stay. A manageable setting, Kolle found.

The Maybachs had insisted on taking advantage of their booked vacation, and Ilona and Franziska had also decided to stay on the hallig. For them, there was no longer any urgent suspicion of a crime. However, they all had to expect that they might be required to appear in court during the homicide trial. It was in the hands of the public prosecutor Eysenhardt to decide.

This evening, they were served a three-course menu that included a so-called salt marsh salad, a Friesian beef roulade with red wine sauce, and crème brulée for dessert. Those who wanted vegetarian could choose between a vegetable curry and Moroccan tabouleh. The drinks were on the house per Budnik's orders.

The guests sat together at a large table, and there was laughter and lots of mutual toasting. Larsson raised an eyebrow slightly when Onne told him about their investigation with exaggerated and embellished details. A clear sign, Kolle remembered, that his colleague from Husum was just as amused as he was.

After dinner, they sat together at the bar, a bottle of whiskey standing in front of them.

Onne cleared his throat and asked, "Can you please tell us who killed Wolters, why and how?"

Kollerup grinned wryly and said, "What's the magic word?"

Onne rolled his eyes and answered, "Please."

Then Kolle filled in all the details: "Jan-Ole was madly in love with Nele. When he was forced to watch as Wolters swept his queen off her feet, he plotted to murder his adversary. It wasn't supposed to look like a murder."

"He learned that ricin, one of the deadliest poisons out there, can be obtained in seed form. Nothing was easier than to purchase a sufficient amount of castor seeds through a completely normal online shop. A handful of seeds is enough to cause irreparable harm to a person. Jan-Ole also ordered the equipment for crushing and pulverizing them online.

"So then, he poisoned Wolters with small doses over several months. He wanted to avoid a sudden fatal dose as much as possible, so that suspicion would not fall on him."

"That's amazing!" exclaimed Onne. "You can just order poison in seed form, no questions asked?"

"Yes, and you can order everything else you might need too." Kolle nodded and added, "You don't even have to go onto the dark web. It's easy to find out how big a lethal dose has to be, how to store the stuff, and so on. If you want to, you can become a murderer at any time, without anyone knowing a thing."

"So how do the Sieverstens and Nele come into play?"

The Inspector was able to explain that too: "The Sieverstens' daughter was killed in a hit-and-run traffic accident in the 70s. The perpetrator was never caught. At some point in the 90s, though, Wolters and the Sieverstens ran into each other at a wedding party. Already three sheets to the wind, Wolters went on and on about how great he was. And he blabbed about some accident he was in as a teenager. The place and time matched what the Sieverstens knew about the death of their daughter.

"For years they lived with this knowledge and finally got to the point that they wanted to incapacitate Wolters on the hallig and let him drown in the sea."

"They just happened to obtain the same drug, purely by chance, as the one Nele planned to use as a weapon.

"Nele wanted Wolters to die, because he had left her even though he had gotten her pregnant. Moreover, he refused to acknowledge his paternity. In her eyes, the only way out of her misery was to murder Wolters.

"Jan-Ole supported her and really egged her on to eliminate his opponent. He concealed from his beloved that he had already been poisoning Wolters with ricin for months. Of course, the small doses had led to unpleasant consequences, but they weren't fatal. The lethal dose he gave Wolters was mixed into the vodka bottle that Nele had enhanced with her medicine."

While Kolle took a sip, there was an uncomfortable pause.

"That means we have four murderers?" Budnik broke the silence.

Kolle nodded. He counted: "Jan-Ole, Kurt and Heidi." He took another swallow. "And Nele," he murmured.

"I'm sure they'll take her extenuating circumstances under consideration," Budnik remarked consolingly.

Kolle waved it off. "Yes, for Kurt and Heidi too, but that's not for us to decide."

"But how did the murder actually take place?" Onne persisted.

Kolle shook his head dejectedly and asked Larsson to continue for him. He was, of course, completely in the picture and could report every detail.

He explained how the Sieversten couple, along with Nele, had poisoned Wolters. The two identical sleeping pills had been combined with the ricin that Jan-Ole had already mixed into the vodka. This mixture of two substances was enough to plunge Wolters into a deep unconsciousness. It was more by chance that Wolters had managed to stagger around half-awake in the storm. It was also an accident that he was struck across the neck by a piece of debris that had caused considerable blood loss. All this together had led to the death of the victim.

Sometime in the early morning, three rather hungover men found themselves sitting on a bench next to the stairs of the hotel, listening to the sounds of "Hotel California," while the sun rose over the Wadden Sea.

A joint was passed around, sweetening the humid air that already carried a hint of salt and summer. A flock of seagulls flew lazily from the mainland and landed in the sheep pasture. A tussle over the best sheep droppings commenced immediately.

"The world can be so peaceful," sighed Kolle.

A twofold approving "Yeah" followed, like an echo.

"Someone else want a beer?" he asked. Two more "Yeahs" followed.

When no one stood up after two minutes, Onne and Larsson looked at each other languidly.

"Who's gonna get them?" asked Onne.

Larsson shrugged and took a drag on the joint. He watched the embers with scientific interest as he slowly exhaled the smoke, before passing the stub to Onne.

"Whoever asks first," was his laconic reply.

"No one's going anywhere," Kolle muttered. He reached

under the bench and pulled out three flip-top bottles. Silently, they toasted each other and watched the seagulls, as the first sheep trotted out of the church into the open air.

It looked like it was going to be a bright summer day.

Acknowledgements

I would like to thank my wife for her patience and insight for accepting my night shifts at the keyboard without complaint.

And I shouldn't forget my cat, Leo, a quiet but valuable co-worker, who spent his nights at my keyboard, keeping me in line.

Of course, thanks also go to my editor Katrin Schäfer. Without her, this book would not exist.

Author's Note

When I had the idea for this thriller in 2016, I was aware that tornadoes can also occur in Germany. I was also aware that these storms can cause considerable damage.

My thought was, "What if they existed in a larger form?" It was only during the course of plot development that I did some interesting research into which tornados we have had to deal with in recent years. One search result led me to an event on the Helgoland dunes. This island off the coast of Helgoland was devastated by a tornado on July 12, 2010. Several people were injured, but the property damage was limited.

Ultimately, not unlike my scenario, this storm could be attributed to climate change resulting in sea warming, which also currently affects the relatively shallow North Sea.

When I was looking for a location for the plot, I immediately thought of the hallig that exists in the North Frisian Wadden Sea: Hooge. Since I didn't want to write a crime novel in which every street and every house was real, I invented Grienoog. This is a Frisian word that means green island. Now you can argue that a hallig is not an island, but I thought the name was quite pretty.

In this crime novel, I touch on two of the important topics here on the west coast of Schleswig-Holstein: the wind power industry and mudflat tourism. Environmental associations and politicians are always involved in the debate about wind turbines. Also, the competitive pressure among the companies is just as tough as that which exists in the mudflat guide field.

Appendix

Characters in the story

Chief Inspector Kollerup, 56 years old
Onne, painter-shepherd, 50 years old

The victim
Kai Wolters, 67 years old, mudflat guide

Hotel workers
Bernd Budnik, 60 years old, hotel owner
Helga Budnik, 55 years old, his wife
Kurt, 23 years old, receptionist and bellhop
Svenja, 30 years old, receptionist and maid, responsible also for the Souvenir Corner
Nele, 26 years old, waitress and maid
Arne, 45 years old, chief cook
Thorsten, 20 years old, kitchen helper
Maik, 33 years old, barkeeper, by day, depending on the weather, at the beach bar, and evenings at the hotel Harbor Bar
Jan-Ole, 57 years old, house technician, oversees the minigolf course

Hotel guests
Ground floor
Room 1 Christa Hansen, 65 years old, retired secretary
Room 2 The Sieverstens, both 68 years old, retired and married
Room 3 No guest
Room 4 No guest

First floor
Room 5 Kollerup
Room 6 Franziska Koch, 30 years old

Room 7 The Maybachs (both about 40), married, with Malte, 6 years old
Room 8 Ilona Schneider, 28 years old

Others
Prosecutor Eysenhardt
Pathologist, forensic pathologist and forensic scientist Dr. Lührssen
Inspector Seigur Larsson, Kolle's "right hand"
Thore Cartensen, Chief of the newly formed Crime Scene Forensics and Evidence Evaluation Division

Brief explanation of some of the special features of the North Frisian Coast. If you want to know more, you can get information from the following institutions:

LKN-SH (Landesbetrieb für Küstenschutz, Nationalpark und Meeresschutz Schleswig-Holstein), Husum or Tönning
Nationalpark-Haus, Husum
Nordfriisk Insituut, Bredstedt
Nordfriesisches Museum, Nissenhaus, Husum

The Halligs
The remains of the original Uthlande area, destroyed by storm surges over the centuries.
There are several theories about the derivation of the term hallig. One of them explains it as a derivation from the Germanic word for salt (hall), which was extracted in this area of Uthlande. It has also been confirmed by numerous scientists that the land has sunken in areas due to excessive salt extraction.
   The second largest hallig with the most inhabitants is Hooge. The largest in terms of area is Langeneß. The halligs are not protected against storm surges by an outer dike and are flooded when the weather conditions are right. The buildings stand, alone or in groups, on so-called terps, artificial mounds of earth that are not yet washed away by the water.

The halligs of the North Frisian Wadden Sea are unique on the globe and are listed as a UNESCO World Heritage Site.

Haubarg

A typical farmhouse on the Eiderstedt peninsula.

After one of the biggest storm tides of the sixteenth century, in which thousands of Frisians died, immigrants coming from the Dithmarschen region settled the then depopulated places in northern Frisia. These settlers brought the construction of the haubarg (etymol.: Heu bergen) with them, which originally had roots in Dutch architecture.

These buildings, with huge storage spaces under thatched roofs, were used to store hay and as a storage place for unthreshed grain. Huge oak trunks enclosed the square, a space also called the gulf. The living quarters and stables were grouped around this framework. The threshing floor, the larder, was located to the side. From here, the harvest was stacked inside the square. The whole farmhouse received its stability from this post and beam construction. If a storm surge ever happened to destroy the outer walls, the upper part would remain intact.

In a haubarg, people and animals lived together under one roof. Not infrequently, haubargs were built on mounds of earth, called warfts. Since at that time there were no or only rudimentary protective walls against high water, this was the only way to protect themselves from a storm surge.

The height of the thatched roof was frequently fifteen meters tall, and the structure had two or three stories. The floor area of most haubargs was approximately nine hundred square meters.

Warft

A warft is a raised mound consisting of clay soil on which the coastal inhabitants of the North Sea marshes built their houses. On average, today's mounds are five to six yards high. The terms kurt, worth or warde are also commonly used for these hills. The term is reflected in place names such as Oldenswort or Witzwort. Often there was only one house on a hallig. Some halligs, like Hooge, have mounds on which several houses stand.

Schobüll

Since 2007, a district of Husum North Sea.

Not without a lot of complaints from its citizens, in 2006, the municipal council of Schobüll decided to become part of Husum for financial reasons. By 2017, the turmoil had settled down. Husum city dwellers like to relax in the beautiful health resort in Schobüll.

Schobüll is the only place on the North Sea coast without a dike, as the village is a breezy six to seven yards above sea level. That is why the Husum district is popular among those who can afford a cottage with a view of Husum Bay. The distance between the two municipalities is only five kilometers.

Husum

The capital city of North Frisia. During the last district reform, the formerly independent districts of Husum, Eisenstadt and Südtondern were merged.

Husum does not have an independent police department, but is subordinated to the police station in Flensburg. In Husum, there is no public prosecutor's office or forensic medical institute with a pathologist.

It has its own district court, though.

Rungholt

Rungholt first appears in the historical record in 1361, when Hamburg merchants were granted the freedom to trade there. According to recent estimates, the village at that time was home to 1,500 to 2,000 inhabitants. Rungholt consisted of several districts and was completely destroyed during the Marcellus Flood, known as the first Grote Mandränke, in January 1362.

Because the inhabitants of Uthland mined the salty peat to extract the salt, the land sank ever deeper below sea level.

To this day, nobody knows exactly where this village once stood. Occasionally, wall remains or wells appear in the mudflats at low tide, or clay shards are found.

Since Rungholt was not the only place destroyed in the storm surges of the fourteenth century, it is impossible to say exactly where this village was located. Although there are maps showing Rungholt, the exact location is not known because these maps were made after the storm surge of 1362.